D1430944

The Magicians

Other books by James Gunn:

THIS FORTRESS WORLD
STAR BRIDGE *with Jack Williamson*
STATION IN SPACE
THE JOY MAKERS
THE IMMORTALS
FUTURE IMPERFECT
MAN WITH A FUTURE, *editor*
THE WITCHING HOUR
THE BURNING
BREAKING POINT
SOME DREAMS ARE NIGHTMARES
THE END OF THE DREAMS

THE MAGICIANS

by James Gunn

Published by
Charles Scribner's Sons
New York

A shorter version of this novel was first published in *Beyond Fantasy Fiction* for May 1954 under the title of "Sine of the Magus."

Library of Congress Cataloging in Publication Data

Gunn, James E 1923–

The magicians.

I. Title.

PZ3.G9526Mag [PS3513.U797] 813′.5′4 76–17558

ISBN 0–684–14782–3

This book published simultaneously in the United States of America and in Canada—

1 3 5 7 9 11 13 15 17 19 C/C 20 18 16 14 12 10 8 6 4 2

Printed in the United States of America

To Jeanne and R.T.
who produced and named Casey

The only trouble with magic is that it doesn't work.

John Symonds

Chapter 1

Magic has power to experience and fathom things which are inaccessible to human reason. For magic is a great secret wisdom, just as reason is a great public folly.

Paracelsus, De Occulta Philosophia

The white letters on the corrugated black board spelled out:

COVENTION

October 30 and 31

Crystal Room

I chuckled. It never fails: hotel bulletin boards are like movie marquees; there always is something on them that is misspelled.

The chuckle died away in the vastness of the hotel lobby like laughter in a church. I glanced around uneasily. My man hadn't come in. I had no reason to be uneasy—no valid reason anyway. I just didn't like the job. Not that it promised to be tough. It was too simple, really, and the old lady was paying too much. And I had the feeling that there were eyes watching me. There was nobody. I could swear to that. And yet I knew I was being watched. That's a switch. It's enough to give any private detective a neurosis.

Hell! Why should anyone pay a thousand bucks just to find out some guy's name?

Wood was crackling aromatically in the fireplace at the far end of the lobby. Easy chairs and sofas were arranged geometrically on a couple of large blue and red Oriental rugs. I made my way across the floor, my shoes going thump-thump, whack-whack, thump-thump, whack-whack as I walked from rug to marble and back again. Then I was at the desk. I leaned against it so that I could watch both doors my man might enter.

The clerk at the desk looked up. He was a type; you've seen him. Thin, thirtyish, dressed in a dark suit and a bow tie, his bald head gleaming brighter than the floor, obsequious to his superiors, vindictive toward those placed under him. Unfortunately, he knew me.

"Hello, Charlie," I said.

"Casey," he said suspiciously. "What are you doing here?"

"Business."

"No trouble, Casey," he said. "I'll have you tossed out of here. The management won't have you raiding rooms, snapping pictures. Our guests pay for service and privacy, and anybody who—"

"Relax, Charlie," I said. "Nothing like that."

He subsided. I felt him sink back from his toes, but he didn't give up. "Since when have you had anything but divorce cases?"

"I've come up in the world, Charlie. Who puts the notices on the board over there?"

"Usually it's the convention management," he said, "but this morning I did it. Why?"

"Can't spell, either, eh?"

He glanced at the board and back at me, his face impassive. "Nothing misspelled there."

"Yeah," I said. "I've always wanted to attend a coven-tion." It started out as a small joke, but when I got to the key word my voice broke and an unpleasant shiver went up my back.

"Now's your chance," Charlie said, "because that's what it is. If you qualify."

"Qualify for what?"

"As a member of the group."

"What group is that?"

Charlie shrugged.

"You mean just anybody can walk in off the street and hold a meeting here?" I said. "For any purpose?"

"Why not?" Charlie said. "They've got as much right as anybody. Particularly if they pay in advance."

"Well, how do I know if I qualify if I don't know what they do?" I asked.

"There's the man in charge now, just coming through the door," Charlie said. "Why don't you ask him?"

I turned my head toward the entrance on my right. Just inside the sliding glass doors, sighing shut behind, was a tall man with dark hair and graying temples. He looked slim and distinguished, though oddly attired for ten in the morning, in evening clothes. In his lapel was a five-pointed star, small, gold, engraved with symbols too small to read from where I stood. The description checked. He was my man.

I started after him.

"Casey—" Charlie began. He was warning me.

I waved a reassuring hand back at him without looking

and followed the back that was disappearing into the dark interior of an elevator that stood open. Above the opening a lighted sign that read "This Car Up" blinked dark. As the man I was following turned around, a heavy brass door closed between us. For a moment, before it closed, he looked directly at me.

His eyes were deep and black and shiny. And I had the foolish notion that they still stared at me through the closed brass door, seeing, weighing, and discarding contemptuously before they turned their shocking intensity on something more worthy of their attention.

The afterimage vanished. I shook myself and looked quickly at the bank of lights which registered the position of every car in the row of elevators. The light moved past M, A, and B, stopped at C, and then continued upward: 4, 5, 6 . . .

I shook myself, pulled my eyes from the hypnotic display, and stepped through the open doors of the car that was identified as the next one to head upward into the mysteries above. The doors closed, and I touched the button marked C. It lit up almost before my finger pressed it, a kind of electronic magic that always surprised me.

We slid silently upward. Bricks alternated with painted metal. The car was filled with the cloying smell of a scented deodorant the management used to kill the scent of elevator shafts too long uncleaned. M, A, B. The first stop was mine. The doors parted in front of me and closed behind me, and I was in a red-carpeted hall facing a cream-colored corridor wall. Painted on the wall in gold was an arrow pointing to my right. Above it were two words: Crystal Room.

I looked to my right. The Crystal Room had double doors,

but only one of them was open. A dark back was just going through it. The young man who stood beside the door, neatly clothed in a camel-colored leisure suit, nodded respectfully to the man who was entering. A gatekeeper. The party was private.

Keeper of the crystal door. Inside was something called a "covention" that sent unreasonable shivers up my back. And inside now was a nameless man—I couldn't mistake that back, as certain of its powers as any emperor—whose name was worth a thousand dollars to me and who had eyes like polished obsidian daggers.

I shrugged the flat automatic in the shoulder holster into a more comfortable position and with that as assurance started after the guy who wore evening clothes in the morning. I nodded familiarly to the doorkeeper, who had broad shoulders, short hair, and a pleasant, sunburned face, and I started through the doorway.

I stopped abruptly, as if I had walked into a glass wall. I rubbed my nose ruefully.

"Where's your name card?" the doorkeeper asked.

I looked at his left breast pocket. On a gummed card, with some other writing around it, a single name was printed: Charon. That's funny, I thought. Charon was the name of the ferryman who took dead souls across the river Styx to Hell; what a name for a gatekeeper. But while I was thinking I said, "Name card?" I snapped my finger. "I knew I forgot something. But you know me. Casey from Kansas City? Met you last year. Don't you remember my face?"

He frowned as if I had said something ridiculous. "How would I remember your face?"

That stopped me. He didn't say he didn't remember my face but that he couldn't; he didn't expect to.

I began rummaging hopefully through the pockets of my brown tweed suit. "Maybe I've got the card in my pocket," I said. There was only one way to go from here—back the way I had come—but I could make it graceful in the unlikely possibility that I ever came back. And then I felt something slick and rectangular in my right-hand coat pocket. Slowly I pulled it out. It was a name card.

The young man looked at it and nodded. "Gabriel," he said. "Wear it from now on. I can't let anybody in without a name card."

I nodded mechanically and walked cautiously into the large room, but the invisible wall was gone. Just inside the door I stopped and turned the card over.

In the center of the card was a circular seal. Imprinted blackly over it were two lines of type.

"Call me GABRIEL," it said, "or pay me five dollars."

That was funny enough, but it wasn't the funniest part. There was no way the card could have got into my pocket. No one could have put it there. The suit had just come back from the cleaners. I had put it on before I came out this morning.

"Gabriel," I muttered to myself. I knew who Gabriel was: one of the archangels. Carried messages. Blew trumpets. That was a hell of a name for a man.

Coventions. Brass doors with eyes in them. Invisible walls. Angels. I shivered. It was getting to be a habit.

The Crystal Room was pleasant enough. It wasn't the biggest meeting room in the hotel, but it was one of the most attractive and it was private. A huge crystal chandelier hung from the center of the ceiling and gave an excuse for the name of the room. Two smaller chandeliers flanked the big one. The ceiling and walls were painted a deep rose and flocked like an old-fashioned whorehouse. The carpet on the floor was burgundy. The hanging crystal picked up rose and red, alternating, blending, flashing as they swayed gently and tinkled together.

A stage had been installed at the far end of the room. It was draped in black like a bier, and black velvet provided a backdrop from ceiling to floor behind the stage. Several chairs were lined up neatly at the back of the stage. In front of them was a lectern. Between me and the platform were rows of wooden chairs; I counted thirteen rows of thirteen chairs each. A few of the chairs were occupied, but most of the people in the room were standing, clustered into small groups, conversing casually or in a few cases with animation. I looked them over carefully, but my man wasn't among them.

The scene was typical of hundreds of professional meetings that take place in hundreds of hotel meeting rooms every day all over the country. Once a year men and women assemble to discuss their single shared interest, to talk shop, to listen to the latest advances in their professions, to raise standards, to elect officers. And to indulge in some heavy drinking, character assassination, and casual—and sometimes not so casual—sex.

The men here were distinguished and well dressed, although none of them were in evening clothes: suits predominated, most of them dark, although occasionally among them was a swinger with long hair and jeans. The women—there were more women than men—were all young and beautiful; not just ordinary beautiful but exquisitely, improbably beautiful. I had never seen so many beautiful women in one room before, not even when I tailed one wandering spouse backstage at a musical comedy. Up close those faces had been a little the worse for greasepaint and the bodies a bit droopy with dissipation. I had the feeling that the faces and bodies I saw here would be as implausibly lovely up close and undressed as they looked from a distance.

But what was their profession? Doctor, lawyer, college professor? In what profession do the women outnumber the men?

If I moved a few steps to the right, I could get a better look at a truly spectacular Junoesque redhead. Like a fool, forgetting my reason for being there, I moved a few steps to the right. My foot caught in something. I stumbled. As I pitched forward my arms reached out for support. They closed around something softly rounded and yielding. It gasped. I looked up into a pair of blue eyes that were crinkled with sudden laughter. I was pressed tightly against a delightful figure.

"You see?" the girl said in a soft, low voice. "Redheads are unlucky."

"For who?" I asked.

"I don't think you will fall down now," she said, "if you should let go."

I straightened and let my arms drop. "I stumbled over something," I said, and looked down at the dark red carpet suspiciously. There was nothing nearby that I could have stumbled over. I would have thought I was tripped but there was nobody nearby except the girl, and she was in front of me.

"It's better to stumble than to fall," she said. "Especially for La Voisin. She's a hag, really. You wouldn't believe. Fifty if she's a day."

I took another look at the redhead. "You're right. I don't believe it."

She shrugged as if what I believed was of no importance. I took a good look at her for the first time. She was only pretty. I might have thought her beautiful somewhere else, but the other women in the room had used up that adjective. Her blue eyes and dark hair provided an interesting contrast, but her features had small imperfections. I know: experts say that imperfections enhance beauty, but her eyes were too large, her nose was too small and turned up a little at the end; her mouth was too generous, and her chin, too stubborn. Now that I was straightened, she reached only to my chin. But her skin was smooth cream—I always found that peculiarly effective in a woman until I found out how much of it comes out of a bottle—and her figure was—well, I mentioned that before.

She seemed to be in her early twenties, which gave her almost a decade on me. The other women didn't look much older, it was true, but there was a maturity to them that showed in the way they stood or moved, and a youthfulness in her that revealed itself in a grin and a girlish slouch. She knew she was being inspected, and she didn't care.

She laughed again. It was a pleasing, girlish sound; it wouldn't flutter any pulses, but it made me want to laugh with her. "Have a program, Gabriel."

She handed me a booklet from a stack beside her. I took it, wondering if her eyesight was unusually good. It would have to be to read my name card. I still had it in my hand. But maybe she had heard the doorkeeper.

I leaned forward to read the name on the card attached to the pleasing slope of her white knit dress.

"Call me ARIEL," it said, "or pay me five dollars."

"Ariel?" I said. "Where's Prospero?"

"He's dead," she said simply.

"Oh," I said. That was the trouble with being an uninitiate in a private gathering. You couldn't say anything for fear of saying the wrong thing. "Thanks for the program, Ariel. And the support."

"Any time," she said. Her blue eyes seemed to say, in a pleasant way, that the words weren't meaningless courtesy.

I started to turn away, pulled by a sense of duty, but a large, jovial man with white hair stood in my way.

"Ariel," he said over my head. "It was sad news about your father. The society won't seem the same."

She murmured something while I glanced at the card on the broad chest in front of me. It demanded that it be called Sammael.

"It's a disgrace that he's got you here passing out programs like a neophyte," Sammael said. "You should be up on the platform with the other dignitaries."

"Nonsense," she said. "I am a neophyte. In spite of what my father was, I'm just an apprentice. Anyway, I volunteered."

"Tut-tut," he said. I listened with fascination, trapped between them without a graceful way to escape. I didn't think anybody said "tut-tut" anymore. "You're an adept if there ever was one. I'd match you against any of them. But I've been out of touch for several months. My own career has arrived at a new crisis point, and I had difficulty getting away even for these two days. But I couldn't miss one of our annual meetings."

"Many of the members have said the same thing to me," Ariel said, "but like you they couldn't stay away. Everything seems to be coming to a focus."

I noticed that she didn't ask about his career, whatever it was. She avoided it as if to ask would be a serious breach of etiquette. "Excuse me," I said, trying to squeeze out from between them.

"Sammael," Ariel said, "this is Gabriel."

The large red face swiveled to inspect me. Blue eyes weighed me; they were ordinary blue eyes, but there was something a little wrong with them, as if they were perfect imitations made out of glass so that they caught the light wrong. "Gabriel, eh? I've heard fine things about you. Great things are expected. Great things indeed."

He'd heard about me? "You haven't heard anything until you've heard me blow my trumpet."

"Exactly," he said. "We're all waiting for that." He turned his blue eyes back on Ariel. "I've been so out of touch, my dear, I haven't even heard how your father died."

"Oh," she said slowly, as if measuring the impact of every word, "he just seemed to waste away."

"Waste away!" Sammael said. The words had connotations that bleached the red face. "Oh, dear. Wasted? Oh, my!" He was backing away as if Ariel had just announced that she was a carrier of the plague. "Very sad. Very sad indeed. Ah well, we all must go. But wasted! Good-bye, my dear. And—" He had been about to say "good luck," I thought, but he had reconsidered and turned away.

I looked at Ariel. She was staring regretfully after the rapidly disappearing white hair. "That's what always happens," she said, "but I had hopes for Sammael."

Just then I saw my man come through a small door beside the backdrop at the far end of the room. He ascended the three steps to the platform and began to converse with another man who had been waiting there. "Who's that?" I asked before I thought, touching her arm. It was a dumb thing to do; if I was a member of the society I should know the others.

"I wish I knew," Ariel said.

"He's a stranger?" I asked, surprised.

"Of course not."

"Then who is he?"

"He's the Magus."

"The Magus?"

"That's what we call the president of our society," she said.

"But what's his name?"

"He calls himself Solomon."

"Or pays five dollars. I know." I sighed and turned away. I would have enjoyed Ariel's company in other circumstances, but I had responsibilities. "See you around, Ariel."

"Good luck!" she called after me.

The seats had begun to fill up, but the back row was still empty. I wandered over and sat down. Overhead the crystal chandeliers tinkled their eternal music. In spite of the fact that I couldn't feel a breeze.

Good luck! Ariel had said. I needed it. I wasn't handling

this assignment in a professional manner. Of course this wasn't an ordinary assignment; every question got the wrong answer. But I was blundering along, giving myself away every chance I got. The girl now—she knew I didn't belong. I'd told her as much several times. But she didn't seem to care. How many others knew?

Good luck? Funny thing: suddenly I felt lucky.

It had all seemed too simple at first. Here's a thousand bucks. All you have to do is find out a man's name.

A name, a name. What's in a name? Gabriel, Ariel, Prospero, Sammael, La Voisin (How did a name like that slip in among the others?), and now Solomon the Magus. I should have told the old lady that. I should have said, "What's in a name?"

Chapter 2

The gates of hell are open, night and day;
Smooth the descent, and easy is the way.

Virgil, Aeneid

I sat there alone in the office for a long time, talking to myself. I'd got in the habit of doing that. It was a bad habit, all right, but there was nobody else to talk to, and it was better than listening to the spiders spinning their webs in the corners and across the door.

The office was small and dark. Just big enough for me and a desk and a filing cabinet with one drawer half full of old file folders and a nearly empty bottle of bourbon. And a chair, now dusty, for prospective clients. Another office, a bit bigger, was on the other side of the right wall. Outside was a water cooler, empty, and a desk for a receptionist and typist, unoccupied. Even the typewriter was gone.

The light that came through the dusty window behind me was that peculiar kind of late October sunlight, pale and a bit spooky, like the sunset over a pumpkin patch, and I sat there, haloed by it, flipping a quarter over and over. It was my last quarter, and I kept telling myself that if it turned up heads I would walk out of the office for the last time and go down and spend the quarter for a cup of coffee and then go to my apartment, get drunk, and tomorrow start looking for some honest work.

But no matter how many times I flipped the quarter, it always came up tails. Finally I let it lie there on the blotter.

Casey, you're a dope.

"You're telling me."

Private detective! Public sucker! You have as much backbone as a jellyfish. You can be talked into anything.

"Don't repeat yourself."

Why waste your life teaching? Start living! Get where the money is! Excitement! Glamour! All you need is a little capital and you can be in business for yourself. Junior partner! Junior moron!

"I know. I know. What can I say? The trouble is: Suzie agreed with him."

He's gone. She's gone. The money's gone. None of them are coming back. It's time you put it behind you. Get out of here. Get a job. Start teaching again.

"Where am I going to get a job in the middle of the semester?"

Get a job, then, where you don't need brains. Because you haven't got any.

I was very hard on myself, and a great second-guesser. But I had good reasons. I stared down at the quarter and thought about a bank account that had been cleaned out and a partner who was in South America or South Africa or South Dakota, and a girl friend who had disappeared at the same time, without a note, without a word, and there was no reason to connect them all together except for the timing but I did. And when I glanced up the little old gray-haired lady was looking lost in the big dusty chair reserved for prospective clients. It was the one respectable piece of furniture in the office except for the desk, and that was somewhat marred by heel marks. The chair, of course, was due to be repossessed any day now.

I must have looked startled. I didn't know how she had got there without my hearing her come in.

"I knocked but you didn't seem to notice," she said.

I doubted that. "What can I do for you?" I asked.

Her faded blue eyes twinkled. You read that a lot, but I had never before seen it happen. I wondered how she did it.

"Before we talk business," she said, "I think I ought to know a little about you." Her face was crackled like old parchment and concerned and kind. An odor of lavender reached me.

I resisted her charm. "I'm a private detective, lady. You get references from butlers."

"At least you don't get any sass," she said. "This is important to me. I just want to ask a few questions."

I sighed. "Okay, lady, ask."

"What did you do before you were a private detective?"

"All private detectives were on the police force," I said. "You learn that from all the detective novels."

"But not you," she said.

I shrugged. "I taught school. High school."

"What did you teach?"

"English, mostly, but I was versatile. I substituted in history and math."

"What kind of math?"

"Algebra, mostly. Occasionally a bit of calculus for the college-bound group." I stopped. I was talking too much. "What is this? What has all this to do with whatever it is you want me to do?"

She smiled at me. "Just a few more questions," she said gently. "It's important to me."

I sighed again and flipped the quarter. It came down tails once more. "Okay," I said. "I'm not going anywhere."

"Why did you leave teaching to become a private detective?" she asked.

"Have you noticed what they're paying teachers these days?" I asked. "Besides, I had a girl friend." I listened to myself with horror. I certainly hadn't meant to talk about Suzie.

"What made you think you could be a successful detective?" she asked.

"You haven't been around any high schools lately," I said. "Actually, I was talked into it. I'm not very good at it, as you can see." I was babbling, and I couldn't seem to help myself. It was as if I was trying not to be hired by this strange old lady.

She nodded, apparently satisfied, and changed the subject. "Do you have any family?"

I shook my head. "I'm all alone in the world."

"Me, too," she said.

I stared at her. Why shouldn't an old lady be all alone in the world?

"We have something in common," she said quickly.

"Yeah," I said, but I didn't like it much.

"You have a girl friend, you said?"

I frowned at this further intrusion into my private life. I decided not to answer and then changed my mind. "*Had*, lady, *had!*"

"There's no one near and dear to you?" she insisted.

"What is it, lady? If I said you were as near and dear to me as anyone on earth, I wouldn't be exaggerating much!"

"It's quite important in affairs of this kind," she said primly, "not to have hostages to fortune whose lives and welfare can be threatened by unscrupulous—"

"What are affairs of this kind?" I asked, and then I realized that in her own old-fashioned way she had told me that there was danger of death and I decided maybe I didn't want to know whatever it was she wanted to tell me.

For she had decided to tell me. She nodded and said, "I want you to find a man."

"Who?"

"If I knew that, I wouldn't need a detective, would I?" she asked briskly.

Why not? I wanted to ask, but she went on before I could say anything. "He'll be coming into the lobby of the hotel around the corner between nine thirty and ten o'clock tomorrow morning. You won't have any trouble recognizing him. I'm sure he'll be tall and slim. His hair will be dark, medium length, graying around the temples. He'll be very distinguished looking. He'll be wearing evening clothes."

"At ten in the morning?"

"Oh, yes. And he'll have a pentacle in his lapel."

"A what?"

"A five-pointed star, made of gold, and engraved with symbols and Hebrew letters."

"He's Jewish."

"I don't think so."

I nodded as if I understood. It was a good piece of acting. "What do you mean, you're sure he'll look like this and that? Haven't you seen him before?"

"Oh, yes. I saw him earlier today. I'm sure he won't trouble to change."

"Change what?" I asked with heavy sarcasm. "His clothes or his face?"

"Either," she said. "But I'm not doing it well, am I?" Her hands fluttered. "I'm afraid I'm only confusing you. Oh, dear!"

Confusing me. That was the understatement of the year. My head was spinning like the gears of a slot machine. I should have told her then that I didn't want her job, I didn't like the sound of it, I didn't believe a word she had said, and I was out of the business anyway, but I looked down at the top of the desk and hit the jackpot. Beside the quarter was a rectangular piece of paper printed green. In each corner was a figure "1" followed by three lovely symbols for nothing. One by one the gears clunked to a stop. This I could understand. I picked up the bill and turned it over. I crinkled it. It was crisp and new and untouched, and I loved the feel of it. "Is it real?" I asked.

"Oh, yes," she said. "It's genuine. And it's yours—"

"How did it get there?" I asked. The pleasure of finding it was wearing off.

"I put it there while you were looking away," she said.

I hadn't looked away from her for an instant, and I knew she hadn't moved. But she said it as if she were telling the truth, and I have heard enough lies from students about absences and late papers to know the truth when I hear it. That was one talent I had for detective work. I looked at the old lady sitting in the big chair, her spectacles sitting on the end of her nose, her eyes twinkling, and before I could say anything else she said, "It's yours if you take the job. Is it enough?"

"To start on," I said, and I was lost. "Let me get this straight. The man you want me to find will be coming into the hotel lobby about ten in the morning— If you know he's going to be there you can find him yourself!"

"That's just the beginning."

"I see," I said, nodding. "You want me to tail him—"

"And make very certain he doesn't know you're doing it. Very certain. He can be dangerous."

"Dangerous, eh?" I stared at the bill in my hand and crackled it again. Maybe it wasn't so big after all. Not that I'm afraid of danger. Not in moderate amounts. I just wasn't sure I wanted a thousand bucks' worth. "So I tail him. And then what?"

"You find out his name."

"His name?"

"His real name."

"I see." This is the first thing I had understood in a long while. "He's going under an alias."

She hesitated. "I guess that's what you call it."

"He's blackmailing you," I said with a scarcely concealed note of triumph in my voice. At least I had figured it out; things began falling into place like the last pieces of a jigsaw puzzle.

She looked shocked right down to the tip of her nose. "Nothing like that!"

"He's involved with your daughter, and you suspect he's married!"

"I have no daughter!" she said indignantly.

I tried once more. "He claims to be a long-lost relative,

and you think he's an imposter." But it was weak, and even I couldn't put any conviction into it.

Her lips pressed together into a single line, like an old-maid schoolteacher I once had who taught handwriting in the fourth grade. She hadn't taught me much either. "Just do what I tell you and don't jump to conclusions. Remember: he's very skillful at—at disguises. If you see him get in a car and see someone get out later looking much, much different, don't be surprised. Believe your own powers of logic, not your prejudices about what you think is possible. Because the man who gets out of the car will be the one you want; it's his name I want you to find out."

"But what if he doesn't get into a car?" I asked.

"That's just an example, silly!" she said impatiently. "You know what I mean."

"I get it," I said. I really did. The old lady was crazy. She had what psychologists call a monomania. She had been looking under her bed for so long that she had started seeing things. And now she wanted to know his name. You might not suspect it, just looking at her, but monomaniacs may be completely normal except on one subject.

I knew what would happen. Nobody would show up in the lobby. I'd hang around for two or three hours, charge her for a day's work, and give the rest of the money back to her. Hell, I rationalized to myself, if I turned her down she might go to someone who wasn't ethical, who would give her a fake name and just keep the whole thousand.

I convinced myself that taking the assignment was the only proper thing to do. I also was hungry, and I thought that I could get a good steak for five or six dollars. "Where will I get in touch with you, Miss— Miss—?"

"Mrs.," she said. "Mrs. Peabody. You won't." She hopped spryly to her feet. "I'll get in touch with you." I got a final faded-blue flash of twinkling eyes as she swept out the door and was gone. I never heard the outer door open or close, but by the time I leaped to my feet and reached the door and tore it open, the outer office was empty. And beyond that the corridor was empty, too. I had wanted to ask her something. I had wanted to ask the name the man was going under, his alias. Mrs. Peabody had really hired herself a detective.

Casey—

"Oh, shut up!" I snarled.

I went back to the desk and studied the bill for a long time. I almost didn't make it to the bank. The bill was genuine all right.

Chapter 3

Oh! My name is John Wellington Wells,
I'm a dealer in magic and spells.

Sir William Gilbert, The Sorcerer

Solomon. That was his name. So what? It wasn't enough to satisfy Mrs. Peabody. There were lots of people named Solomon. I knew one myself. Sol the Tailor. But Sol the Tailor had a last name. I didn't know it, but he'd tell me if I asked him, I'm sure. What's your last name, Sol? *So who wants to know?* Just curious. *So it's Levi; maybe that makes your day?* But already I had the feeling I didn't want to walk up to this tall, slim man dressed like a magician in a tuxedo and ask him for his last name.

But how do you go around without a last name? You don't go up to a person and say, "I'm Solomon." Not unless you want the other person to reply, "And I'm the Queen of Sheba."

Somewhere his last name was recorded.

I looked down at the program. It had a shiny black cover. Across the top, in letters dropped out of the black and then overprinted in red, it said:

THIRTEENTH ANNUAL
COVENTION OF THE MAGI
October 30 and 31

In the middle of the cover, left white, was a seal. It was an odd-looking thing with two concentric circles enclosing what looked like the plan for an Egyptian burial pyramid. Not the pyramid itself, but the corridors and hidden chambers and transepts, or whatever they're called. To hide the body and its treasures from the grave robbers. The scent of the grave, of something musty and rotting, seemed to drift upward from the program. In the corridors and between the two circles were printed letters in a foreign alphabet. I thought it was Hebrew.

There was something familiar about the seal. Then I remembered. I looked at my name card. The same seal.

I leafed through the program quickly looking for names. There weren't any. Usually the officers are listed somewhere in a program booklet—the president, the program chairman, the people who get the complaints when things go wrong—but there were no such lists in the booklet. Apparently this was so close-knit a society that everybody knew everybody else. At least by their first names.

But like all programs this booklet had advertising. There is something about advertising that is more revealing than all an organization's statements of purpose, as if what someone thinks the members want to buy says more than what the members think they do. But I must admit that the ads puzzled me.

One ad was illustrated with all sorts of engraved five-pointed stars, crudely drawn stars, stars in double circles with cryptic lettering, and some circles with no stars at all. The message said: "PENTACLES OF GUARANTEED EFFICACY. Consecrated. Guaranteed. Satisfaction or your money back. P.O. Box 2217 . . ." Some of the pentacles were described as "pentacles to gain love," "pentacles to influence good spirits favorably," "the Great Pentacle," and "talismanic pentacles."

Another ad touted a book entitled *One Hundred Spells for All Occasions. Revised, with Mathematical and Verbal Equivalents Printed Side by Side for Easy Reference.* "Every spell," it said, "has been tested under laboratory conditions and has been proved effective." This ad not only offered money back but consulting services "at cost."

Pentacles? Spells?

The Thaumaturgical Book Shop advertised a long list of books which could be purchased at prices ranging upward from one hundred dollars. All were listed as manuscript copies. I let my eyes travel down the column of titles:

The Grand Grimoire
The Constitution of Pope Honorius
The Black Raven
D. Joh. Faust's Geister und Hollenzwang
Der Grosse und Gewaltige Hollenzwang
Le Dragon rouge, ou l'art de commander les esprits célestes, aériens, terrestres, infernaux

Farther down the list shifted into Latin:

Magia Naturalis et Innaturalis
Sigillum Solomonis
Schemhamphoras Solomonis Regis
De Officio Spirituum
Lemegeton

At the bottom, all by itself, was *Clavicula Solomonis.* "The true *Key of Solomon.* In his own hand." That was priced at ten thousand dollars. At that it was dirt cheap. These people were in the wrong business, whatever that business was. A manuscript copy of a book written by Solomon himself would bring millions in the rare book market. I shook my head. These were obvious fakes, but they all took themselves so seriously. Either it was all the most straight-faced put-on I had ever seen, or everybody in the society was mad.

I skipped over the page of the day's program, saving that for later, and continued looking through the ads. You never realize the fantastic things you can buy until you chance upon a specialized booklet like this. I once stayed at a hotel that was having a convention of beer-can collectors, and I was told that a rare, old can sold for one hundred fifty dollars. Empty.

magic wands (cut from virgin hazel with one blow of a new sword)
quill pens (from the third feather of the right wing of a male goose)
arthames (tempered in mole blood)
black hens and hares (for haruspicy and spells)
nails (from the coffin of an executed criminal)
bat's blood
tail of newt
candles made of human fat
hands of glory
hemlock, henbane, black hellebore, Indian hemp
coriander, liquor of black poppy, fennel, sandalwood
aconite, belladonna, peyote, virgin papyrus, mercury
magic sieves (for coscinomancy)

The list went on and on like the offerings of a chemist's

shop or an old-fashioned country store located in Transylvania. Maybe, I told myself comfortingly, these people were illusionists, and the ads were a kind of extended practical joke, tracing the ancestry of these prestidigitators back to their medieval predecessors, the alchemists, the sorcerers, the witches and warlocks. . . . This was a professional organization for stage magicians. The names they used were their stage names. That was what it was, I told myself. That was what it had to be.

But I didn't like the explanation. It didn't explain too many things.

I turned back to the list of the day's activities. Something was wrong with it, but I couldn't figure out what it was. Then I realized. It was a two-day meeting, but the program covered only one page, and it was headed October 30. Where was the program for October 31? I searched through the booklet in vain for another page before I decided that my booklet must have been defective.

I read the list of the day's activities:

OCTOBER 30

10:30 SPELL and GREETINGS by the MAGUS
10:45 WITCHCRAFT—A DERIVATION
10:50 SAFETY IN NUMBERS: THE COVEN
11:00 CONTAGION—WHY SPELLS ARE CATCHING
11:30 IMITATION—THE SINCEREST FORM OF SORCERY
12:00 CALCULUS: THE HIGH ROAD TO BETTER FORMULAE
12:30 POSSESSION—NINE POINTS OF THE LORE
1:00 Recess
3:00 PRACTICAL USES FOR FAMILIARS
3:30 THE ELEMENTS OF THE ART (with examples)

4:00 ALEXANDER HAMILTON'S CORBIE
4:30 LYCANTHROPY—A DEMONSTRATION

The item about lycanthropy stopped me. Sweat was dripping down my sides and the sweat was cold. I knew what lycanthropy was. It was people turning into werewolves. And these people were going to demonstrate it. They were crazy, all of them, and the sooner I was out of this place the happier I was going to be.

"You don't belong here," someone said softly into my left ear.

I looked around. Ariel was sitting beside me, her head close to mine. In other circumstances I might have enjoyed it. Now I drew back a little. "You're telling me!" I said, and then quickly changed it to, "I mean, why do you say that?"

"It doesn't take genius to figure that out. You didn't know Solomon, our Magus. You walk around staring at everything as if you had never seen it before. And I happen to know that Gabriel is dead."

I shivered. I had assumed the name of a dead man, and I felt as if someone had measured me for a coffin. "Did he waste away?" I asked. My voice was shaky.

"No, he was hit by a car while he was crossing a street." She looked as if she were concerned about my welfare. "But you don't need to be alarmed. I don't think anybody else knows about his death. It only happened two days ago."

"That isn't what I was alarmed about," I said. I was wearing a dead man's card; maybe it wasn't unlucky but I wasn't going to wait around to find out. "That does it," I said, standing up. "I'm getting out of here."

She yanked me back into my seat by my coattail. "Sit

down," she whispered, looking at the people sitting around us. "You'll attract attention, and that could be dangerous. Don't try to leave now. They'd get suspicious. And they don't take chances. I won't give you away. Wait until the recess, and then you can walk out inconspicuously along with everybody else."

I pointed a shaky finger at the program. "But this is—this is—"

She looked at me, and her eyes were wide and blue and innocent. "It's only magic."

"Magic! Real, honest-to-God magic?"

"Of course. What did you think it was?"

Magic? No, that was impossible. I couldn't accept that. Madness was more like it. And for me the only question was who was crazy: Ariel, the others, or me? She didn't look crazy. The rest of them didn't look crazy. They looked like handsome, intelligent people gathered together to discuss their profession. Whatever it was. Not magic. Oh, no! Not in the nineteen seventies. Not in a big metropolitan hotel surrounded by the everyday details of transient life, by bellhops and maids and waiters and people coming and going. Not with the sun shining and cars in a traffic jam outside and people working and eating and sleeping and going to football games and watching television and making love.

Spells and magic wands and graveyard dust. Witchcraft and formulae and sorcery.

"Ouch!" I said.

"What's the matter?" Ariel asked.

I rubbed my thigh. I was awake, all right. That was bad

news. If *I* wasn't asleep and *they* weren't crazy, then *I* was the one who had gone round the bend.

But I didn't feel crazy, just baffled and bewildered.

And then the man called Solomon the Magus was on his feet, standing behind the lectern. Solomon the Magus. Not Solomon Magus. I began to understand a little more. Magus was his title, and the Magi were the society. He was the Magician of the magicians, like the Shah of shahs. Magus was the singular form of magi. Magicians all.

Everyone was seated. All the seats were filled. It was strange, I thought. Nobody was absent because of illness or the press of business or any of the other reasons which kept people away. Not even death, I thought, remembering Gabriel. Maybe nobody *dared* to be absent. Something might happen while they were gone; something might happen to them *if* they were gone.

Against the black drape Solomon's face and triangular expanse of shirt front floated unsupported in space, and his disembodied hands hovered in the air for silence. Silence fell.

He began to speak. His voice was low and resonant and clear, and I couldn't understand a word he said. His fluttering hands gestured a strange accompaniment like pale butterflies in a mating dance. He finished, smiled, and then launched into a general welcoming speech to the society that I understood perfectly and wished I hadn't. It could have been repeated word for word to any professional gathering anywhere in the country.

Ariel leaned toward me. "The first thing he did was an Egyptian spell," she whispered. "A standard thing—asking that we be blessed every day."

"Damned decent of him," I growled, but the sarcasm was to hide the fact that I did feel happier. Well, not happier exactly. There was a better word for it, but I didn't want to use it. Blessed.

The first four speakers on the program were as dry as only the learned can be when they are discussing their specialties in front of other specialists and wanted to be careful not to appear unsophisticated and unprofessional. Even the audience of initiates grew restless as the speakers expounded their technicalities and quibbled over minutiae.

All except me. I sat in a state of shock. They were being dull about magic. They were being pedantic about sorcery. Behind everything they said, justifying their dullness and their pedantry, lay a pragmatic belief in the existence of magic as a physical, usable force. It was like a seventeenth-century man walking into a meeting of electrical engineers or an early-twentieth-century man listening to the discussions of scientists talking about getting power from the atom.

One of the speakers demonstrated, etymologically, that witchcraft, though long derided and denigrated, is the art or craft of the wise. Another pointed out the significance of the medieval satanist groups of thirteen, which were called "covens," and why their annual meeting had been named as it was this year. And he called their attention to the fact that the room held thirteen rows of chairs and that each row had thirteen chairs in it and that the number of people in attendance was exactly one hundred and sixty-nine—a coven of covens.

The audience murmured about that. Neighbor looked at

neighbor. Ariel stirred beside me. "I don't like this," she said. "I was afraid this might happen."

She was afraid. If she was afraid, what must I be feeling? I felt it.

If I had not been dazed by a continual bombardment of the impossible, I might have come out of the meeting with a liberal education in the theory and practice of magic. The next two speakers went into it thoroughly.

The layman's concept of magic as mystic symbols and arcane language as a means of controlling unseen, sometimes demonic, forces was at best an oversimplification. Actually the magician's view of the world was the poet's view: they both saw things in terms of metaphor and image and analogy and inner logic. All the universe is implicit in every piece of it, they both said. Blake wrote:

To see a world in a grain of sand
And a heaven in a wild flower,
Hold infinity in the palm of your hand
And eternity in an hour.

And the scientist has said, "Give me a molecule and I will predict the universe." So the magician says, "Everywhere things are alike. The universe is mirrored here on earth. We can learn about God's plans for man by studying the simplest expressions of his intentions. Or by studying the movement of the stars and the planets we can predict events that will happen to individuals."

And since man is made in God's image, we can learn about God by studying man. That was the goal of the alchemist: not just to turn base metals into gold, or to discover the elixir of life, but to know God.

"As above, so below." This was the enduring theory of magic. As things were in the skies, so they were on the earth. And similarly, "As below, so above." What one could learn on earth applied to the spiritual realm and the whole universe.

Thus spells worked on two principles, by contagion and by imitation. Contagion associated ideas by contiguity in space or time. Objects that once had been in contact with others always were in contact with each other, like hair and nail clippings, which retained an association with the person on whom they once had grown. What was done to them was done to the person.

Imitation associated ideas by similarity. An effect could be produced by imitating it. If you wished to make rain you sprinkled water in the dust. Pope Urban VIII had a magician make him a little universe with lamps and torches inside a sealed-off room in order to avoid an eclipse the Pope feared would signal his death. An image—a wax doll, a mommet—would transmit to the person with whom it was identified whatever was done to the image.

But while it was going on, the picture was not that clear. Terms swirled in my head. Demonstrations went on in front of my eyes. Spells, rites, the condition of the performer. Faith and works. The reservoir of psychic powers. The doctrine of opposites and the Mysterious One which unites them. Sexual vigor. Cleansing rites. The names of power. Spirits, demons, and the magic circle.

Twisting columns of smoke ascended from the platform and assumed subhuman faces—the faces of demons, the speaker said—with hateful, leering expressions. A beautiful girl without a wisp of clothing materialized out of the air and posed for the audience before disappearing. One speaker looked around for a drink of water and when none was available snapped his fingers and a tall, cool drink appeared on the lectern.

At times it was all I could do to hold onto my seat with both hands.

The next to the last speaker on the morning program climbed slowly to the stage from the floor. For some reason he had not been given a seat with the rest of the speakers. He was a little man with rosy cheeks and a fringe of white hair encircling a bald spot that gleamed pinkly from the stage as he bent over a thick, bound manuscript.

He looked out over the audience hopefully, nodding to the smattering of applause, and read a few introductory paragraphs in a high, sprightly voice. His thesis was that developments in higher mathematics had made psychic phenomena truly controllable for the first time in history. He implied that the society had been founded on this theory, that its purpose had been to develop the theory into a workable science, and he suggested that these things had been allowed to slip overboard—if they had not been purposefully jettisoned for something darker and less significant.

The audience murmured. There was a note of uneasiness in it, as if a mild-mannered man had put down his glass in a bar and suddenly announced that he could lick any man in the house. I looked at Solomon's face, but it hadn't changed expression. The speaker peered over the lectern benignly.

"Who's that?" I whispered to Ariel.

She was sitting up straight, her eyes studying the reaction

of the audience. I thought she looked disappointed. "Uriel," she said, and sighed.

Ariel, Uriel. Was there a connection?

In spite of his perceptions of the ways in which the society's direction had been altered, Uriel said, he had moved ahead with the research as originally planned, and he now proposed to give the society a summary of his results.

He asked for a blackboard, and—like every other lecturer I've ever seen—he had trouble getting it onto the stage. Two young men struggled with it, stumbling, juggling, catching their feet on unsuspected projections. The audience began to laugh at their antics, and then at Uriel. Uriel endured it all with beatific patience.

When the blackboard was finally in place, it blocked Solomon and the previous speakers from the view of the audience, but the board seemed to have a life of its own. It kept jiggling and jumping while Uriel was trying to write on it.

The audience laughed again.

Uriel stepped back and turned his head to scan the upturned faces below him. He sighed as if he were accustomed to this sort of thing. "We have practical jokers," he said. "That is quickly remedied. You are all familiar with the usual verbal formula"—from the blank faces around me I suspected that they were not as familiar with the verbal formula as Uriel supposed—"which sometimes works and more often does not. Mathematics, the language of precision, does it like this."

He drew two crude arrows on the blackboard, pointing

toward the floor. It was not all that easy to write on, the way it was moving around. Above the arrows he scribbled a formula that looked familiar to me, filled with elongated *f*s and little triangles which were, I supposed, the Greek letter delta. The moment Uriel wrote down the last symbol the board settled down solidly on its feet like a mule determined to move no more.

"Now," he said, like a patient professor with a backward class, "let us proceed."

And then he launched, unfortunately, into a history of the calculus, beginning with Newton and Leibnitz, which bored everyone in the audience except a few who may have been professional mathematicians. And me. My college mathematics came back to me. The idea that Uriel was trying to get across to his audience was fascinating in its concept and even more so in its implications. Magic as a science and mathematics as the key tool. This was the first thing I could really understand.

"The merit of calculus," Uriel concluded, "is that it expresses concisely and accurately what verbal equivalents only approximate. Accuracy is what is needed for the proper control of the magical forces—accuracy and limitation. How many times have you summoned something—a glass, say—from the kitchen, only to have your table littered with glasses. Accuracy. Accuracy and limitation. If you wish to improve your formula, know your calculus!"

And he turned to the blackboard, scribbled a formula on it, and the blackboard disappeared. Just like that. Without smoke, curtains, or illusion. I blinked. The applause was perfunctory. Uriel nodded, his bald head beaming pinkly, and trotted off the stage.

Ariel was clapping enthusiastically beside me.

"They didn't seem to like that very much," I whispered to her.

"Oh, they're too lazy to learn anything that complicated, and some of them just aren't very bright. It's a wonderful help, really, and Uriel's a dear, getting up every year and trying to help them. And they just laugh at him behind his back."

Solomon announced that because the morning session had run long—every program I have ever been a party to has run long—the lecture on possession would be postponed until the afternoon session. But those who had not sneaked out during Uriel's talk were already getting up to leave. The morning session was over; it was time for lunch. I walked, dazed, into the corridor with Ariel. I didn't believe it. I tried to convince myself that I didn't believe it. But I had heard it and seen it. It was true. These weren't illusionists with their tricks and distracting patter. They were the real thing. In the last quarter-century of the twentieth century. They practiced magic, and it worked, and they held conventions, just like veterans and dentists and lawyers and economists and physicists and a thousand other groups and professions.

And nobody suspected. They were less suspected than if they had met atop Brocken on Walpurgis Night.

Chapter 4

The chief enemy of life is not death, but forgetfulness, stupidity. We lose direction too easily. This is the great penalty that life paid for descending into matter: a kind of partial amnesia.

Colin Wilson, The Occult

"Ariel!" I called. "Ariel!" She was getting away from me, and she was my one bridge to reality. "I've got to talk to you." She hesitated and then turned back. I was getting fond of the way she looked at me.

"My consulting fee is high," she said.

"How much?" I asked.

"A steak," she said. "About that thick." She held out a finger and a thumb about two inches apart.

"For lunch?" I asked. "I thought girls were supposed to be on diets, eating salads with no dressing, things like that."

"Not this girl," she said. "Magic uses up lots of energy."

I looked at her quickly to see if she was joking, but I couldn't tell. She didn't look like a witch; she looked like the girl who lived next door. Prettier, maybe. That kind of witchcraft I could handle. "Okay," I said. "I guess the budget can handle that if you can handle the steak."

Fifty people were waiting for the elevators. "Let's walk down," Ariel suggested.

I held open the door that opened onto the gray stairwell, and we started down anonymous gray steps.

"What's to keep me from telling the world about the strange things I've seen here today?" I asked abruptly. "And what would happen to your happy little society if I told?"

"The answer to both questions," she said, "is: nothing. Who'd believe you?"

"Nobody," I said gloomily. I knew what would happen. *Magicians? In the Crystal Room? Witchcraft? Covens? Spells? Sorcery? Sure, Casey. I know just the person who should hear all about it. Come along. Come along quietly. Don't get violent.* "The crazy thing about it," I said, "is it works. Why do you keep it hidden? It would be worth millions if you could bring it out in the open. Patents. Services."

"If you had a mint," Ariel asked, "would you rent it out?"

"I don't understand."

"The members of our society are the most successful people in the world," Ariel said. "Why not? They're one up on everybody else." Her voice sounded a little bitter. "They are businessmen and lawyers and politicians, a physician or two, nurses, actors and actresses, entrepreneurs, gamblers, maybe politicians, and for all I know kings and queens. If their normal abilities don't get them ahead, they can always use the power. They can jinx the opposition, bless their own enterprises, use spells, perform rites, change their appearances, heal the sick, win the case—"

"But people like that I'd recognize!" I protested. "Their pictures would be in the papers; they'd be interviewed on television; they'd be on talk shows—"

"I told you they could change their appearance," Ariel said. "If you could see them as they really are you could recognize half of them, I'm sure. The last place any of them would want to be recognized, however, is here. Of course we can make some guesses about people in the world who are unusually lucky, who win success far beyond their abilities. But nobody knows for sure; good fortune may strike without the intervention of magic; some people have a natural pipeline to the psychic reservoir."

I thought of a world in which the richest, most powerful men and women were sorcerers, and shuddered. "But I thought magicians and witches were—"

"Ugly people who lived in poverty and filth and waited for people in need of their services to come skulking around to their huts or tents?" She laughed. "Why should initiates wait to be paid by other people for making them rich or loved or powerful? It never did make sense."

"That's right," I said and awoke to the fact that we had been walking down these steps for a long time. I looked down the way we were going and saw the steps continuing downward without turning until they vanished in the murky distance. I looked back the way we had come. The steps went up and up, unending. The walls were smooth and gray and unbroken.

I turned to Ariel in panic. "What's happened? Where in the hell are we?"

"Oh, dear," she said, looking around. "You may be right. About our location. It looks very much like a trap."

"A trap?"

"A kind of maze," she said. She caught my hand and patted it. I would have felt more reassured if I had not felt so much like a child. "There's really nothing to get alarmed about," she continued. "It's very simple. We'll just have to sit down until I can get my bearings. People have starved in these, of course, but there's really no danger in them as long as you keep your head."

That was easier advice to give than to take. I did not react calmly to the notion of starving to death on these stairs.

She sank down on a step. I collapsed beside her. For the first time in years I wished I was back teaching *Silas Marner* to reluctant students.

Ariel took some objects from her purse and put them down on the step beside her: colorless lipstick, some eye makeup, fingernail clippers, keys, pen, checkbook, penlight, and assorted junk. Finally she turned the purse upside down and shook some bobby pins out of the bottom. She replaced the rest of the objects and began to bend the bobby pins. "Talk if you wish," she said, her hands busy. "It won't disturb me."

"How—" I began, and then started again. "How long have people been able to do these kinds of things?"

"Not long. Not unless you count the Chaldeans and the Minoans. They were said to have magicians, but we can't be certain. Of course there are legends and myths and folk tales; some reality may lie behind them, no matter how slight. If we believe them, magic has been part of human experience since man first began to personify natural forces and see spirits in all living things. Death released those spirits to wander around; they could be used for good purposes or bad, and natural forces could be controlled."

What if the myths were true? I asked myself, credulous for a moment, and then I rejected all such possibilities. That was nothing but superstition. What I was concerned about was some new kind of science. "I mean the kind of things I saw happening up in the Crystal Room."

"That was magic, too," she said. "You'll never understand it unless the evidence of your eyes can dent your hard-headed materialism. And until you understand how this side of man has been suppressed by science and technology, how doing things with one's mind and hands replaced mysticism as a search for truth and power. Because there was a search down through recorded history. The wisest of men pursued it, believed in it, even testified to their success. The alchemists seeking not just the philosopher's stone but God. Responsible men like the Dutch physician Helvetius, a German professor, Wolfgang Dienheim, and the Swiss philosopher Jacob Zwinger all testified to seeing gold made before their eyes."

I thought about it and found the whole narrative pretty unconvincing. That kind of success could have changed the entire history of Western civilization. The reason we had rejected magic for science was that all evidences of the success of magic were deception—or self-deception, delusion, mass hypnosis . . .

"You're probably asking yourself why it didn't catch on if it was so successful," she said. I started, but she went on without noticing. "It must have been a haphazard business, this searching after secret power, and those who stumbled on the right formula or procedure believed that they were uniquely blessed, the chosen, the elect. They didn't want to share their discoveries with their neighbors, even if they could do so without being feared or hated, accused of witchcraft or demonology. They might hint at it—for they were human enough to want to seem brave and powerful—but they wouldn't ever set anything down except in parable and symbol. Their knowledge would die with them. Secrecy became a way of life. Everyone had to start from zero."

Secrecy could explain a lot of things, I thought. But it was also a good way to hide the falseness of superstition.

"In *The Doctrine and Ritual of Magic,* Eliphaz Levi wrote, 'To attain the *sanctum regnum,* in other words, the knowledge and power of the magi, there are four indispensable conditions—an intelligence illuminated by study, an intrepidity which nothing can check, a will which nothing can break, and a discretion which nothing can corrupt and nothing intoxicate. TO KNOW, TO DARE, TO WILL, TO KEEP SILENCE—such are the four words of the magus. . . .' Of course he went ahead and wrote about them."

"In the program," I said, "a lot of old books of magic and spells were advertised. If secrecy was so important—"

"They couldn't keep entirely quiet about it," Ariel said. "Human nature being what it is, they had to boast a little, to hint that they had been in personal contact with God or Satan and had forced them to do the magician's will. But those who did write about their successes, who weren't outright fakers, or self-deluded fools, put them down in such cryptic language that nobody else could duplicate their work until my father and Uriel began experimenting with mathematical equivalences."

"Your father and Uriel were the discoverers of the new art, then," I said. I was getting nervous sitting here on these gray anonymous stairs, but talking was better than thinking about it. "How did the rest of those unscientific people get into the group? What happened to secrecy?"

"This isn't the Dark Ages, you know," Ariel said. "And my father and Uriel belonged to a different tradition. They were both mathematics professors at a large state university, and Uriel wanted to give it to the world. He wanted to publish their results in a mathematical journal. It would make them famous, he said."

Famous! I thought.

"He always was a bit unworldly," she said. "But they were only junior faculty members. They had no reputations as scholars, and Father told Uriel they would just be laughed at and locked up. He was always much more practical and decisive, and he convinced his brother-in-law, my uncle. A few tricks wouldn't convince anybody, he told Uriel. Illusion, they'd say; or hypnosis."

My face felt hot. I had thought of that myself in my need for explanations.

"Father wanted everything investigated and documented before they disclosed anything. So he and Uriel recruited a few trusted friends and formed the society to compare results and present papers and decide policy."

I looked down the stairs receding infinitely and thought that hell was not hot and red but gray and unchanging. "Nice friends," I said.

"It wasn't the first members," she said. "Most of them are gone now. The society grew. It got out of hand. One member would present a friend of his for consideration. Some members died and were replaced by others—all without anyone knowing, we think. And there always have been a certain number of practicing magicians and witches in any period. Not adepts, you understand, but aware of the power and able to get results occasionally. The society was broadcasting a lot of psychic energy. Magic does that, you know. It has to get energy from somewhere. Uriel has been speculating recently about an alternate universe, in another dimension. When that energy is released, it sets off vibrations if you're sensitive to that sort of thing."

The sort of feeling, I thought, *that one gets walking into a haunted house or by a cemetery at midnight. Or just the feeling of power, the charisma, around certain people.*

"The practicing magicians and witches demanded that they be admitted to the society," Ariel said, "and Father decided it would be better to have them where they could be watched and where they would have to obey certain rules of behavior for the use of the Art. But—"

She stopped. I looked up and saw her eyes filling with tears, and I remembered that her father had died, perhaps recently. As I watched, one tear spilled over and ran down her cheek. I handed her my handkerchief. She wiped her eyes and smiled at me as she handed it back. She looked very appealing at that moment, and I would have done a great deal to keep tears from ever clouding those blue eyes again. I stopped short of magic.

"That was silly," she said.

"Not at all," I said. I wanted to put my arm around her and I did. It felt good, and she seemed to like it there. "Go on if you can."

"I'm all right," she said, and after a moment she continued. "It didn't work out the way Father planned. Gradually the others took control and turned the society in other directions. Instead of a professional society, it became a social group without any real power. Now the Art is being used for all sorts of personal gratifications. Well, last year Father, as Magus, proposed that it was time to make the Art public. Private research had done as much as it could, he said. The Art could best be furthered by general participation and discussion."

In spite of all my earlier doubts, I began to imagine all the ways in which the Art could be used to solve our problems. It could extend our medical resources, maybe even cure diseases now considered beyond treatment. It could solve our energy problems; it could clean up pollution. . . . I imagined snapping my fingers and sending all the junk thrown out of automobiles right back into those cars, removing the chemicals from the streams, taking the soot and lead and various oxides of sulfur and nitrogen out of the air and depositing them where they could be reused. It could eliminate radioactive wastes. It could feed and clothe the poor, maybe even educate the illiterate, perhaps even help the disadvantaged nations of the world to achieve a standard of living that would encourage them to control their own birth rates, all without industrialization and pollution and using up scarce resources. . . .

"Father was voted down," Ariel said. "So he gave the members an ultimatum. He would give them a year to think about it. If they didn't come up with a better proposal in that time, he and Uriel would reveal the Art."

"And then?" I asked, but I knew the answer.

"He died a month ago."

"Murder?"

"He just seemed to waste away," she said. "Come on."

She got up. My arm fell away. In her hands was a V-shaped wire made of bobby pins bent and hooked together. She held the two ends, muttered something under her breath, and walked up a few steps holding the wire horizontally in front of her. Or maybe, I got the uneasy feeling, it was pulling her.

She stopped and turned toward one blank gray wall. I scrambled up after her. She moved her hand against the wall as if she were removing condensation from the inside of a window. An opening appeared in the wall. We looked out through it into the lobby as if it were a pane of glass or a one-way mirror.

People were streaming out of the elevator. I didn't recognize anybody I had seen in the Crystal Room. But I did recognize some of them. One was an energy multimillionaire; I had seen his face on a recent cover of *Time*. Another was the most recent Hollywood sex goddess, only from here she looked neither like a goddess nor particularly sexy. A third was a country rock star whose talent escaped me but who was capable of sending audiences into spasms of enthusiasm. A fourth was a notorious gambler whose winnings at every kind of game had made him internationally famous. A fifth was a man reputed to be in charge of all Mafia operations on the East Coast. A sixth was a woman whose predictions had made her syndicated columns popular in several hundred newspapers. . . .

I recognized about half the people passing through the lobby, and I felt as if I ought to know about half of the remainder. "Are these your members?" I asked Ariel in a whisper. I didn't know whether it was necessary, but it felt appropriate.

She shrugged.

"Is any of them Solomon?" I asked.

She shrugged again.

"Why do they appear to us like this?" I asked. I was getting frustrated with questions for which I could find no answers.

"I don't know," she said. It seemed to me that she was speaking the truth; she was really puzzled. "It may be a trick to throw us off. It may be an illusion like the bottomless stairs. Or it may be real. Under certain conditions—reflections in mirrors, for one—people are shown the way they really are. Maybe my counter-magic has acted like a mirror. In the area of spells and counter-spells, we have a great deal yet to learn. The most important thing to learn, however, is that you can't trust anything."

"Or anyone?" I added.

"Or anyone," she said. And added, gratuitously, I thought, "Including me."

A moment later we stepped into the lobby. By then the others were gone, and I had no opportunity to notice if they changed into someone else. The lobby was only a lobby, the plain, everyday, ordinary place I had left a few hours before. The wood fire was still scenting the air. People were walking purposefully toward exits or from them, or seated on a sofa talking to others, or reading a newspaper in one of the armchairs. I didn't recognize any of them.

I looked back the way we had come. The open stairs went up to a landing, turned, and ascended toward the mezzanine. I faced Ariel. My knees were trembling, but I managed to keep my voice steady. "What would have happened," I asked, "if we had just kept going down?"

But she refused to speculate. "It was just an illusion, you know."

Ariel got her steak. It was broiled, rare, and she ate with enthusiasm, which in other circumstances I would have enjoyed. My appetite was gone, and I was able to get down only half a hamburger before my stomach announced that it was unused to these kind of carryings-on and would cooperate no more.

In spite of all my problems, I found myself watching Ariel, and I realized that so soon after Suzie I was growing fond of the girl. Suzie had taught me nothing. But Ariel was so different. Suzie had been more beautiful, but Ariel was prettier. Moreover, Ariel was pleasant, warm, talented, and she seemed to be interested in me when she didn't have a steak in front of her.

I was beginning to wonder if she was interested in temporary arrangements when I remembered what her talent was. A man doesn't want to walk out on a witch; that sort of thing could be permanent, and I resolved to put any such thoughts out of my head before she sensed them. I had the feeling that she was good at that as well. "People don't just waste away," I said.

She shook her head. "There are lots of ways to kill a person with magic. The old books are full of them, and some of them really work. You don't even have to believe in them, or know about them. Everybody has heard of wax dolls and pins, but dolls—sometimes they're called mommets—can also be made out of clay and left in a stream; and if the mommet has a connection with a real person the person will slowly die as the doll dissolves."

"What kind of—of connection?" I asked.

"If you know the person's real name and call the doll by it, for instance. Or if you have hair or fingernail clippings or handwriting or a photograph or a recording—anything associated with the person."

"The law of contagion," I said.

"That's right," she said in surprise. "How did you know that?"

"The program this morning," I said gloomily. "I learn. I learn slowly, but I do learn."

She was thoughtful for a moment as if she were remembering some painful experience. "Just before he died, Father told Uriel that somebody had said a Mass of St. Secaire for him. But by then his mind was wandering."

A Mass of what? I thought. I would never get everything straight. They kept pulling new terms on me.

"A Black Mass," Ariel said. "Sometimes it's described as the customary mass that's said for the dead, but it is said for someone who isn't dead—yet. Sometimes it includes all sorts of demonic reversals. You know, like inverting the cross, starting the Lord's Prayer with 'Our Father who wert in heaven.' Instead of the Host, they eat and drink all kinds of vile substances. Sometimes they copulate on the altar, kill animals, some say human children, all sorts of nastinesses that I hate to think about, much less describe—"

I was trying to understand the kind of people who would do these things, not just for fun but seriously. "Why would people with such power descend into those kinds of perversions?"

"For some of them it's part of the process of getting the power," Ariel said. "For others it's a religion. The Cathari and the Albigensians were still powerful religious sects in twelfth-century France before the Pope declared a holy crusade against them, and a vast army of Christians swept down on southern France to wipe out whole towns, heretics and faithful alike, with plenty of rape and plunder. And what the crusade didn't destroy, the beginnings of the Inquisition mopped up."

"But—a religion—" I began. To me there was only one religion, Christianity with all its splintered faiths which, along with atheism, provided opportunity for any variety of conviction to find a home. To me the other religions of the world were just a kind of exotic playacting, often with costumes and strange architecture and peculiar fascinations.

"The Cathari drew much of their beliefs from the Gnostics and the Manichees," Ariel said. "They believed that the Old Testament God was a demon, that the world was the creation of the Devil, the Monster of Chaos, that physical existence was evil, that it should be ended as soon as possible, that people should not have children. Many of their practices ended up associated with witchcraft."

"You—you believe in this sort of thing?" I asked, fearful of an answer even here in the polished plastic and chrome of the coffee shop. Ordinary people were going about their ordinary concerns, waitresses clanked dishes and silverware and snarled at the customers, the air was filled with the smell of potatoes and meat and coffee, and I was back in the Dark Ages with heretics and the Inquisition.

"Of course not," she said. "That's all superstition. But other people believe it, and they act upon their beliefs. You see, witchcraft and magic have two separate traditions. One believes in the worship of the Devil and his demons; it practices pollution, sacrilege, desecration, violation, and other kinds of filth. The other believes in the ability of the human mind to command secret forces, in compelling them to do the bidding of man through knowledge and moral force."

Yeah, I thought. *Black magic and white magic.*

"To call them black and white is an oversimplification," Ariel said. "Every magician believes that his magic is white."

"Every one?"

"Well," she admitted, "maybe not every magician. Like ordinary people, some of them enjoy sadism and degradation. Anyway, my father told Uriel that he had been wrong. He said they should have given the Art to the world as soon as they had demonstrated that it worked."

"Or, better yet, burned it," I said gloomily.

"My father said that, too," Ariel continued. " 'I'll break my staff, bury it certain fathoms in the earth, and deeper than did ever plummet sound I'll drown my book.' But he was out of his head then and had confused himself with his namesake. He and Uriel had agreed long before that this was no solution. Real knowledge is indestructible. Someone else would have discovered it. Somebody less scrupulous. Like some of the people who wormed their way into the society."

My mood had changed from that of a half-hour before when I had imagined all the possible benefits of a world in which magic worked. It wouldn't be that way at all. Instead, every man and woman would suspect his neighbor of working secret evil against him or of succeeding beyond his own abilities. There would be no public laundries or barber shops or manicure salons unless they were carefully guarded and every item and clipping protected. Nobody would allow pictures to be taken or records to be made. Birth certificates would all have to be destroyed, and files of all kinds containing names. Devils would lurk everywhere; no one's property or person would be safe; wars would be fought with regiments of demons, battalions of zombies, and batteries of spells and curses. Nothing would be real but hate and fear . . .

"My father and Uriel used to discuss what kind of world it would be where magic was as common as electricity," Ariel said. "They agreed it wouldn't make that much difference. People would learn to live with it in the same way they learned to live with the airplane and the automobile and television, and soon it would provide a new source of power to improve the conditions and the potential of humanity."

"Like making people waste away?" I suggested.

"Father always was so careful," she said. "He burned his nail clippings and hair combings. Of course we didn't know much about this sort of thing. We weren't interested in experimenting in that area, Gabriel, but some—"

"My name isn't Gabriel," I said. "You know that. It's—"

"Sh-h-h," she hushed me, holding up her hand for emphasis and looking around at the people seated nearby. None of them seemed interested in our conversation. "You mustn't speak your real name. Anyone who knows it has power over you. That must have been what happened to Father. Several people knew his name. Many of them knew where he had taught; most of his career was a public record. Someone must have mentioned it."

"To whom?"

She looked cautiously around the coffee shop again. She lowered her voice. "To Solomon. He's always been Father's rival, and he was the leader of the group that opposed making the Art public. And now that Father is dead, Solomon has made himself Magus. No one will ever again suggest releasing the Art."

"But couldn't anybody talk? Couldn't you and Uriel publish an article or tell the newspapers or stage a demonstration or—"

That frightened her. "Oh, we *couldn't!* You don't know what Solomon could do if he had an excuse! He could mobilize the entire society against us if he could convince the members that we were a threat to all of them. Only Father had a chance of defying Solomon, and he's dead. Did you notice how feeble Uriel looked today? I'm scared, Gabriel. If something happens to Uriel, I'll be all alone."

"But if you knew his name," I said slowly, "you'd have a weapon you could use against him. You could protect yourself."

"That's right," she said eagerly. "Could you do that? Could you find out his name for me, Gabriel? I'd pay you. I'd—"

"What do you think I am?"

She paused as if she were considering the question for the first time. "I don't know," she said quietly. "What are you?"

"I'm a private detective," I said. "I follow people and discover things they'd rather hide. But I have a client."

"It isn't Solomon, is it?" she asked quickly.

I thought about it for a moment. "No, it isn't Solomon." And then I reconsidered. "At least I don't think so."

"Then couldn't you do this, too? What does your other client want you to do?"

"The same as you."

"Then it wouldn't hurt to tell me if you find it out, would it, Gabriel?" she said urgently. "Please, Gabriel." Her blue eyes were anxious on mine. I looked into them as long as I dared.

"I guess not," I said. I never could resist blue eyes that looked trustingly into mine.

She breathed again. "Who is your other client?"

"I'm not supposed to tell you that," I said, "but I guess it doesn't matter. I don't suppose it's her real name, or maybe even her real appearance. It's a Mrs. Peabody. A little old lady. Know her?"

She shook her head impatiently. "It could be anybody. We all go under assumed names when we're together, and most of us change our appearances, too, so that we won't be recognized."

I thought of something for the first time. "You mean you don't really look like this?"

"Oh, not me," she said. She smiled innocently. "Everybody knows me."

I wanted to believe her. "That makes it tougher to pin down Solomon. No name. No face. If we assume he's American, male, and adult, we only have about fifty or sixty million people to choose from." Suddenly I snapped my fingers and got up.

"What's the matter?"

"Idea!"

I breezed into the lobby and up to the desk. Charlie

looked up respectfully, but his face fell into more familiar lines as he recognized me.

"The fellow who told you how to put that notice on the board," I said. "Is he registered here?"

Charlie scowled at me. "Tricks?" he said.

"No tricks. Scout's honor."

"Penthouse," he said.

"How'd he register?"

Charlie pulled out a drawer and leafed through a block of cards. He flipped one out on the desk. I looked at it hopefully. Then my hopes sank into the pit of my stomach. In bold black letters on the card was printed the name "SOLOMON MAGUS."

He was bold and confident. He flaunted himself and his society in the face of the world, sure of its blindness. But did his daring approach the foolhardy? Was he getting over-bold, overconfident? It was a key to his character. Maybe it would be the key to his downfall.

"You let him sign the register like that?" I asked.

Charlie shrugged, sorry now that he had let me talk him into a breach of confidence. "Why not? He had a credit card with the same name."

"Thanks," I said, and went back to Ariel. "What was the meaning of that trap on the stairs?" I asked. "Why did they do it?"

She put down her coffee cup. It had no lipstick stains on it; I liked that. "That was a warning, I think," she said.

"To you or to me?"

"I'd thought it was to me," she said slowly. "But now—"

"Yeah," I said. "Be good or be dead."

"What are you going to do?" Ariel asked, her eyes fixed on me as if I were the most important person in her life.

I had been wavering before. I liked to tell myself that I was another Philip Marlowe and trouble was my business. I drew the line at magic and witchcraft. Not now. I wasn't really tough. I was just mad. "I don't like warnings," I said.

Chapter 5

GLENDOWER: I can call spirits from the vasty deep.
HOTSPUR: Why, so can I, or so can any man;
But will they come when you do call for them?

William Shakespeare, Henry IV, Part 2

Ariel said that it would be safer if we weren't seen together. I didn't like that. I argued that we had already sat through the morning session, had been seen talking in the hall and in the lobby and eating lunch together, and whoever set the trap on the stairs knew more about us than either of us liked. But her caution prevailed, and I sat through the afternoon program alone. It made a difference not having a comforting presence beside me.

I was more attentive and more frightened. Magic. It was real and prosaic, and the latter was the more frightening of the two. Magic was a casual, everyday thing, done by the light of the sun; they accepted it, like the water that comes out of a pipe when you twist a faucet or the lights that turn on when you flick a switch, like the voice that speaks from a telephone or the face that appears on a television set.

A middle-aged man with brown hair and a neat brown goatee talked about familiars and their practical uses. An unseen hand turned the pages of his manuscript; a glass raised itself to his mouth when he stopped for a drink of water. I thought to myself that it could have been done just as easily, and perhaps with less effort, by hand.

"Proof!" shouted someone from the audience.

Solomon was beside the speaker, lean, dark, and compelling, as if he had materialized on the spot instead of moving forward from the row of chairs at the back of the platform. "Will the person who spoke stand and make his objection clear?"

Uriel stood up in the front row. I saw his pink bald spot gleaming from where I sat near the back. "What proof does the speaker have of the existence of familiars? Where do these mysterious creatures come from? How do they exist? Why should we postulate them when there are simpler explanations—?"

"You've just seen—" the speaker began, motioning toward the glass and the manuscript.

"Telekinesis," Uriel scoffed. "Anyone here could do the same things without summoning a familiar."

The leaves of the manuscript fluttered wildly and then tore themselves into small pieces and fell around the speaker like a paper snow. The glass rose in the air and poured its contents onto the rostrum.

"Child's play," Uriel snorted.

"I ask simple courtesy for our speakers," Solomon said, frowning. It was an obvious play to the audience considering what had happened to Uriel during the morning session. "What point do you wish to make in this disruptive fashion?"

"I wish to register a protest against the trend of this 'covention,' as you insist on calling it. Covens. Familiars. Is this the type of research the society should approve? Where are your controls? Where is your evidence? What are your hypotheses and how do you propose to test them? Is what we have seen today the kind of investigation the society was set up to consider? I'm afraid it's little more than medieval superstition."

A murmur ran through the audience. I couldn't tell whether it was approval or protest.

"Then you do not believe in the spirit world?" Solomon asked with quiet malice.

"No, sir," Uriel said. "I do not. And I do not believe in slipshod investigations and wild surmises without the slightest shred of scientific evidence. I ask for a vote of disapproval."

The audience was suddenly silent. Solomon looked out over Uriel's head with dark, cold eyes. "Is there a second?"

The silence was broken by a single small voice, a voice I recognized. "I second," someone said. It was Ariel.

A brief smile twisted Solomon's thin lips. "All in favor say aye."

Two voices were raised. I sat back, silent and afraid.

"It seems," Solomon said, smiling more broadly, "that the motion has failed."

He returned to his seat with what may have been a more normal method of travel.

Alexander Hamilton's corbie turned out to be a cat, and Hamilton an English witch, in Lothian. The speaker, a strikingly handsome woman, tall and slender with a silver streak across her black hair, used the corbie as a takeoff point for a general summary of divining and augury. Undaunted by his previous defeat, Uriel arose to protest against the unwarranted assumption that the future can be known and that the ideas of divining and augury had any validity.

"If we can know the future," Uriel said, "then the future must be fixed; but if the future is fixed, what good does it do us to know what is going to happen if we cannot change it? What good to know when we are going to die, if nothing can be altered? What good to know the ill fortune that lies ahead if we cannot avoid it?"

"Ah!" the woman said, "but we can! That is the importance of augury and divining. We can change what we do not like."

Uriel beamed as if she had fallen into his verbal trap. "If the future can be changed, then it is unreadable; there is no future to be read. And all your peering into the entrails of slaughtered animals, all your haruspicy, stichomancy, necromancy, cascinomancy, geomancy, lecanomancy, and crystallomancy are nothing but frauds or self-delusions. Present your proof. Your proof!"

He sat down triumphantly, but Solomon appeared at the podium once more and thanked Uriel for his contribution. The audience chuckled. It was obvious that whatever prestige Uriel had enjoyed was vanishing under Solomon's treatment.

"Now," Solomon said, "perhaps in the next two demonstrations we can give Uriel some of the proof he has been demanding."

I realized, with a shock, that the next speaker's subject was "Lycanthropy—a Demonstration." He was a large, confident man with implausibly red hair. He brought props with him: some unusually shaped lights which were plugged in but not turned on, and a dark, frightened young man whom he installed in a chair at the back of the stage.

After going through a historical discussion of the werewolf and the geographical distribution of recorded incidents, he described his exhaustive research into the facts which lay behind the reports. In one of his own classes he had found a subject who confessed to strange appetites and stranger dreams. One evening, by the light of the full moon, the speaker saw the subject change.

In order to perform this demonstration at times which did not coincide with the proper phase of the moon, the speaker had duplicated with these lights the constituent part of the moonlight which stimulated the remarkable cell changes. He motioned the young man to the front of the stage. He came forward with the gait of a sleepwalker.

"Watch carefully!" the speaker said. And he flicked on the lights.

The young man was bathed in silver, and Uriel was on his feet, protesting the inhumanity of this kind of demonstration. But Solomon's voice was loud and implacable. "Uriel has been demanding proof. Now, it seems, he does not want it after all."

Then the growing murmur of the audience drowned out both of them. The proof was in front of them: the young man was changing.

His dark face grew darker and sharper. His jaw thrust forward horribly. As his arms and legs shriveled and shortened, he dropped to all fours. He was hairy. He shook himself free from the encumbering clothes, and the wide mouth in the pointed muzzle opened to let a long tongue loll out between sharp, white teeth. His eyes gleamed redly in the light. A growl started deep in his throat. He crouched.

A woman screamed.

The wolf sprang. He sprang straight for Uriel.

In the midst of shouting and scurrying and the crash of upset chairs, people leaped aside. Uriel stood straight and unafraid, a small, white-haired figure, oddly epic and alone. He pointed a finger at the descending animal and muttered something I couldn't hear.

The animal crashed into an invisible wall. It dropped among the chairs, tried to get up but failed, and lay among the splintered wood snarling at its left hind leg. The leg was obviously broken. The wolf whimpered as it touched the leg with its muzzle. It was a strange, pitiful sound.

Uriel bent over the creature and marked a few symbols on the floor with a piece of chalk. Instantly, without transition, the wolf turned back into the young man. He was naked and white, and his face was twisted with pain.

Crouching beside him, Uriel drew a broken line on the floor, marked out a mathematical formula, and joined the broken line with another chalk mark. A look of dazed relief spread across the young man's face. He felt his leg with a gesture of disbelief. It was no longer crooked.

Uriel helped the young man to his feet, whispered a few words in his ear, patted him on the arm, and motioned toward the door. The young man turned, gathered up his clothing from the platform, and left, glancing back with distaste and defiance at the man who had been his professor.

Uriel's face, as he turned it toward the stage, was stern. No one had moved during the entire episode, and his voice broke the silence. "Lycanthropy indeed! A psychological state associated with hysteria is more like it. In this case, abetted by hypnosis and sorcery. The Malays often induced lycanthropy in persons of extreme suggestibility; they were called *latah*. Well, these latter-day savages will torture that boy no more."

The audience was shaken, but no one spoke. Uriel turned back toward the platform. Solomon was standing beside the podium, silent, perhaps disturbed, though it was difficult to tell. "What further dark demonstrations do you have for us?" Uriel asked.

Solomon seemed to hesitate and then to make up his mind to push ahead. "The final demonstration," he said, his voice calm and unmoved, "is the one held over from this morning's program. A practical proof of the presence of demons."

I shivered, remembering the item from the morning's program. Possession.

A young man came up to the platform followed by a girl of about eleven. The man was classically handsome. He had shiny dark eyes and white teeth, and he looked uncannily like that movie star of the thirties or forties, Tyrone—Tyrone Power. The girl was cute and pretty at the same time; she had brown hair and freckles and a turned-up nose, and she was wearing an attractive short blue dress as if she were going to school.

The young man held the little girl by the hand and talked about demons and the ways in which they took possession of people. Sometimes they did it because the people were evil or had bargained their souls away, but sometimes they did it to anybody, innocent or guilty, capriciously. It seemed unfair to me, like the story about the man walking by the cemetery at night; he begins to feel nervous and imagines that a foul fiend is walking behind him, and then he consoles himself by saying that if the powers of darkness could work their will on a person like him, who was good and upright and God-fearing, why there wouldn't be any justice in the world. And a voice behind him said, "There isn't."

Like the man in the story, I found that difficult to accept. Sure, Mephistopheles might drag off poor, protesting Doctor Faustus, but Faustus had sold his soul to the Devil and just wanted to back out of the deal. But I didn't want to think we lived in a world where innocence could be raped by evil and we could not protect ourselves. I never liked the story of Job, either.

By the time I got back to listening, the speaker was talking about the devils of Loudun. He described how demons had taken possession of several nuns in the Convent of the Ursulines, including the Mother Prioress herself. With the little girl standing trustfully by his side, the young man described the pact with Satan that the priest of Loudun, Urbain Grandier, had written, which still could be viewed in the Bibliothèque Nationale, along with other documents relating to the celebrated case, including the remarkable deed written and signed by the demon Asmodeus when he was dislodged from the body of a nun by Father Jean Baptiste Gault. He went on to tell how the nuns confessed to intercourse and other unnatural acts they had been forced to commit with Grandier because the demons who possessed them had made them do so, and how the demons were exorcised by Reverend Père Surin. The demons who possessed the Mother Prioress, he said, were named Leviathan, Balam, Isacaron, and Behemoth, and Behemoth was the last one to be driven from the holy Mother's body.

I had heard something of the story before, but this time the telling was subtly different. I had the feeling that the speaker and his audience were on the side of the demons.

For one moment the schoolgirl was standing beside the speaker at the podium, neat and demure, and the next moment she had changed into something else, something terrible and revolting. Her body contorted itself into inhuman shapes. Her arms waved like snakes, and her head twisted itself on her body. Some horrid creature stared boldly out through her face, shouting obscenities at the audience in hoarse bellows that could not have come from that small throat. When the coarse, masculine voice stopped for a moment, vomit spewed from the girl's mouth, and then the obscenities began again.

Suddenly I believed in demons.

"Get a priest!" someone shouted.

"Asmodeus!" the young man called out. "Are you there? Speak to us! Tell us about the demon world! Tell us about spirits and the underworld and the great mysteries—"

"Isn't someone going to help that poor girl?" I heard someone scream from the rear of the audience. I thought it was Ariel.

"Speak to us, Asmodeus!" the young man repeated. "Say something to prove that it is you!"

Uriel was standing in the front of the platform. He was writing rapidly on a piece of paper braced against his left hand.

"I—AM—AS-MO-DE-US!" the girl said in a deep, impossible voice. "The cow is mine."

Uriel had finished writing. He held up the piece of paper, waving it as if to attract attention, and then set fire to the paper with a cigarette lighter in his right hand.

"This bitch will do as I order—" the voice that called itself Asmodeus began and suddenly began to scream as if it had been set aflame.

The girl fell silent. She looked around at the audience with frightened eyes, as if she was aware of where she was but she didn't know how she had come there. But I knew, and everyone knew, that the demon was gone.

The audience seemed to emit a collective sigh. And then everyone looked at the young man who had led the girl to the platform, who had called upon Asmodeus to communicate. Now he was silent, but he seemed as if he had clamped his lips shut over a terrible compulsion to speak. His face reddened, his eyes bulged, and then a great, terrible shout of pain and terror burst from his mouth, and he leaped from the stage and ran, staggering and bumping into chairs and walls with strange fury, until he reached the closed glass doors of the Crystal Room. He burst through them. The glass fell in pulverized fragments behind him, and he disappeared, bleeding and screaming, down the distant hall.

"There are no demons," Uriel said softly, but his voice seemed to fill the room. "There are only delusions and deluded men. The source of the Power is neutral. Electricity is neutral; it can provide light or warmth, or it can project pornography and kill."

He turned to the audience. "Will you approve this wanton display of vileness and cruelty, too?"

The audience moved uneasily, but no one spoke. Most of the people glanced toward the stage, where Solomon leaned against the lectern. They seemed to expect a response from him, but Solomon stared down calmly, undisturbed.

Uriel swung back to the platform, a finger pointing at Solomon. The Magus straightened quickly. Uriel laughed. "You needn't worry. I won't use my power against my fellow man except in self-defense." Uriel gave the last words peculiar emphasis. "You think you are wise. You are foolish. You think you know everything. You know nothing. As the surviving co-founder of this society, I disavow the leadership. I disavow the society. And I leave you this thought to consider: I will not permit the Art to be used for evil!"

He turned and stalked from the room, small and defiant and somehow wonderfully courageous. Following him was Ariel. She was leading the frightened little girl, an arm comfortingly around her shoulder, whispering into her ear.

At the door Ariel turned. "You cowards!" she said at all of them. Including me. And yet, just before she and the little girl hurried after the little mathematician, I thought her eyes met mine with an unspoken appeal.

What did she want of me? That I find out the name of the mysterious Solomon? Or something more?

While I puzzled over it, the meeting broke up. Some of the members walked toward the door. They were in little groups, some sheepish and silent, others talking excitedly. A few gathered around the stage, around Solomon. The redheaded La Voisin was among them. Her figure was as magnificent as ever; her hair was striking; her face was exquisite; everything about her promised gratification. But she no longer appealed to me. Something inside me was comparing her with a girl who was only pretty but who had something La Voisin lacked—not just those indefinable qualities of goodness or purity but something more indefinable, a kind of reality.

Too late, I noticed that I was sitting all alone in the room except for the group at the platform. It was too late because Solomon's intense black eyes that looked as if they could bore holes through armor plate were fixed on me even while he was talking to the others. What a great detective I had turned out to be! Not only did I not make myself unobtrusive, I was as obvious as possible.

Solomon broke off his conversation. "Sir," he said, not raising his voice but projecting it at me so that it seemed to come from a few feet away. Some skilled public speakers have that ability without the use of magic. I filed that bit of information away, just like a real detective. "Sir," he repeated, "we would be honored if you would join us."

Join them. It was the last thing in the world I wanted to do, in either sense, and perhaps the last thing in this world I would end up doing. On the other hand, to break for the door would be the worst kind of cowardice. And, with the kind of powers I had seen demonstrated in this hall, perhaps useless.

"The honor," I said, "is mine."

I walked toward the stage, trying to assume a debonair saunter and a confident tilt of the head, and afraid that I merely looked foolish. I had the uneasy feeling, kind of a crawling of the skin, that I was being inspected by four men and a woman, both outside and inside. I felt chilled by it all. But the woman's eyes held a kind of personal inquisitiveness that made me colder than all the rest.

No matter what the ordinary dress of the five people at the front of the room, no matter what the casual interest of their ordinary faces, no matter what the polite shambles of the meeting room, I was approaching a kind of witches' summit, a devilish ceremony in which I would be expected to play the central role. I steadied myself with the thought that at least they lacked the proper numbers; they didn't have a coven.

"Gabriel, eh?" Solomon mused when I was close enough for my badge to be read.

La Voisin looked surprised. "But I thought—" She stopped abruptly and looked at Solomon.

I was glancing at her name card. I had to stand almost on tiptoe to read it because the magnificent slope of her bosom tilted it virtually horizontal, but I made out the first name. "Catherine." Catherine La Voisin. I was no wiser.

"You thought what, my dear?" Solomon asked, beating me to the question.

"I thought Gabriel would be a much smaller man," she completed smoothly. Her eyes narrowed and her pupils expanded to suggest that I was also much sexier than she had imagined; it was like being plunged into a steaming bed and wondering if one were going to escape alive.

It wasn't what she had been about to say, however. We all knew that.

"Well, Gabriel," Solomon said, "what is your opinion of this afternoon's activities?"

I weighed being noncommittal and discarded it. Perhaps it was the feminine challenge of La Voisin. Perhaps it was only the appropriate decision that boldness might win me points. "It looks like Uriel has won the battle," I said, "but you haven't lost the war."

He smiled with real amusement. I awarded him a kind of grudging admiration. He was a good antagonist; nothing shook him. He seemed to enjoy crossing words with me. Or maybe he was contemplating the fate he had in mind for me. I knew I was in the presence of pure evil.

"The sides have been chosen," he said. "The body of the society against an old man and a young girl. The program was intended to accomplish that one event. Uriel has cut himself off from the society, and the society will have to act to defend itself against the threat he represents."

Whether that was Solomon's intention or not, he would never admit to anything else.

"The question is," he continued, "where do you stand in this conflict?"

"Where I have always stood," I said bravely.

"Just who are you for?" La Voisin broke in.

I looked at her and smiled for the first time. "For myself, of course."

"Of course," Solomon said, leaning lazily against the lectern, enjoying his superiority in height as well as knowledge. He gave La Voisin a quick, reproving glance, and she went into a shell of silence. "But in this case self-interest should ally you with the side that is certain to win. There can't be any doubt about that. At the risk of being ridiculously melodramatic, we must put the matter bluntly: we insist that all those who are not for us are against us."

I shrugged, feeling better about my ability to hold my

own, at least until he resorted to arcane powers. "That's understandable," I said. "But in a situation like this, superior numbers do not always indicate superior forces. It seems to me that the issue is still uncertain."

Solomon's eyes bored at my head. "Your name seems to place you on the side of the angels. But names have ceased to mean much any more. My admiration for your independence and your spirit would torment me if we were forced to strike blindly. Perhaps—permit me to suggest it—you might give us some reason to trust you."

"Like what?"

"Like, say," he appeared to consider the matter, "like your real name."

"Certainly," I agreed. I studied the waiting faces of the group around me—the young man, the middle-aged man, the distinguished older man, the red-haired witch, and Solomon; I imagined them stripped of their clothing and their civilization dancing in a kind of religious frenzy around my paralyzed body while somewhere in the darkness that surrounded the terrifying scene lurked something awful and indescribable, waiting for the ceremony to end so that it could feed. And then the vision faded, and they were waiting for me, clothed, polite, but underneath their veneer as savage as hyenas. "Providing you give me the same reason to trust you," I continued smoothly. "Starting with"—I let my eyes roam around the group—"starting with you, Magus."

Solomon laughed. "You are a clever man, Gabriel—and a brave one. Speaking only for myself, I hope you choose the right side. It would be a pity to—lose you."

I controlled a shiver. "Losing" was a euphemism I didn't

like the sound of. "When the time comes," I said, "you'll find me on the winning side."

I nodded to them all, turned, and left. I walked quickly toward the door, feeling their eyes boring into my back like .38 slugs, expecting something strange to happen to me, like changing suddenly into a bat or a beetle or a blob, or suddenly ceasing to exist.

"Gabriel," someone said huskily behind me as I went through the doorway into the corridor beyond.

I jumped and turned, shivers running up and down my spine as if some mad xylophonist was hitting my backbone with icy mallets. The red witch, Catherine La Voisin, was gliding toward me like the figurehead on a pirate ship.

"Gabriel," she repeated, giving each syllable a seductive value of its own. She stopped her progress toward me only when she was close enough to be behind me with another half-step. "You interest me, Gabriel. There is something very real and male about you."

I tried to tell myself that she was the kind of person who would be interested in anything real and male, but it didn't work. She had focused the full warmth of her femaleness upon me, and I could feel myself drowning in it.

"Could it be," she began. "Are you—perhaps—undisguised?" She pressed closer.

"I—I mean—that—wouldn't be—" I tried to get it out but couldn't. Two firm, oversized cones were trying to bore their way into my chest.

"I like you, Gabriel," she breathed. My eyes glazed, as if I were wearing glasses and she had fogged them. Her lips came toward mine.

I looked at them as they approached me like rippling red

snakes, fixed like a frightened rabbit in frozen anticipation. The lips blurred. My gaze shifted upward to her eyes. They were bottomless, like dark blue lakes fading in the remote distance into black.

Her lips met mine. They tingled as if they were charged with electricity. They moved. They parted and her perfumed breath entered my mouth. My arms automatically went around her. Her flesh was soft under my hands. I felt her hand work up the back of my neck into my hair, pressing me closer to her. After a moment I began struggling for breath.

After an eon, she moved slowly back, her eyes heavy lidded and sleepy as if she had just awakened. I drew in a deep, harsh breath.

"What was that?" I gasped.

She was walking away from me down the corridor. Her head turned to look back over her shoulder. "That," she said, smiling confidently, "was a preview."

An elevator door opened in front of her as if she had summoned it, and she stepped into the car. As the doors closed she was still looking at me, and her smile was strangely and disturbingly triumphant.

Chapter 6

The universe is full of all kinds of energies. Matter is energy—the most resistant and uncompromising kind of energy. And if life has succeeded in achieving some degree of conquest of matter, is it absurd to suppose that it has not succeeded with more malleable forms of energy?

Colin Wilson, The Occult

I breathed deeply again, gradually freeing myself from the spell—natural or unnatural—she had thrown over me. Before, in spite of myself, I had been overwhelmed. If there had been a bed handy, I would have tumbled into it in spite of something screaming within me that I would hate myself after it all was over. Now I felt unclean. I pulled out my handkerchief and scrubbed my lips with it. The three men who had been with Solomon passed me, smirking. I glared at them. When I took the handkerchief away, it was stained with orange smears, and the three men were gone.

I waited a few minutes more, but Solomon didn't come out. Uneasily, a bit timidly, I glanced into the Crystal Room. It was empty. Very empty. The room felt hollow. The chandeliers had stopped tinkling. I wondered if the experiences I had undergone in the past few hours had begun to develop in me a kind of psychic sensitivity, or whether I was, at last, gaining the awareness that every private detective needs if he is going to succeed.

In spite of my confidence, I walked uneasily through the Crystal Room toward the only other door. It was in back of the platform, and it was closed. I hesitated in front of it and then slowly, silently, turned the handle and eased the door toward me. I stiffened myself for a shock, but the little room beyond was empty too. An ice-making machine muttered to itself and suddenly showered a tinkling of crystals into its bin. Opposite the door in which I was standing another doorway, with swinging doors, opened into a large central kitchen and serving area. I went to the doors and looked in. The kitchen was empty; the stainless steel was sterile; only the vague memories of old banquets remained. From the kitchen naked stairs led down to other floors.

I turned back to the little room with the ice-making machine. I couldn't see the elegant Solomon trotting down the serving stairs. But he hadn't come out the main door either. Not unless he had come through disguised as the invisible man. He had either gone through here or—but speculation like this was futile. I decided that it was time I stopped playing someone else's game—magic—and started playing my own—detection—such as it was.

I looked around the little room. Solomon had been here. Maybe some of the others, too. They had waited here before they came onto the stage, maybe discussing the program, their findings, their strategy. There should be some evidence of their presence. Besides the ice maker, the only object in the room was a coat rack. It was empty. Bare metal hangers, battered refugees from too many closet encounters, hung from a bar from which olive-green paint had been scratched. The floor was bare plastic tile, a weary, mottled yellow. Idly, I moved the coat rack a few inches and noticed a small, rectangular piece of paper on the floor. I picked it up. It was a ticket on the airline shuttle to Washington, D.C. It was dated day before yesterday, but it hadn't been used. It was still good.

I shrugged. Maybe, maybe not. I slipped the ticket into my coat pocket and searched the rest of the room carefully. I even looked into the bin of the ice-making machine, but there was nothing in it but ice. I took out a cylindrical piece and stuck it in my mouth. It was cold and real.

I went back into the Crystal Room and looked on the platform and around it. Just as I was going to give up, I noticed a small, yellow triangle sticking out from under the black drapes behind the platform. I pulled it out. It was the corner of a piece of yellow typewriter paper. It was bound together with about seventy-five other sheets of paper by a black binder. It was a manuscript, and someone had written on it, in a precise, readable script. But I couldn't read it. Most of it was mathematics. On the first page, for instance, was this:

$$\lim_{\Delta X \to 0} \frac{f(X + \Delta X) - f(X)}{\Delta X}$$

I recognized that much, anyway. It was part of the calculus which Newton and Leibnitz had invented, independently, to deal with problems concerning rate of change. This particular formula had to do with the "derivative," an abstract limit. I remembered that much from my college courses and the occasional ones I had taught in high school, mostly as a substitute. If I thought about it, more would come back. I didn't know what the manuscript was trying to say, but I knew whose it was. It belonged to Uriel.

There was nothing else under the platform or in the room except a couple of rolled programs and some assorted debris. I went out into the corridor with the manuscript under my arm and waited ten minutes for an elevator. It would be months before I could trust stairs again. I wasn't too sure about elevators, either. They could go down faster and farther than stairs, I supposed, but I knew about stairs, and the elevator descended the normal distance in the normal time and I stepped out into the lobby. At least, I thought it was the lobby. The way the normal things of life were changing around, I couldn't be sure. I wondered if this was how the world was going to be from now on.

Charlie was off duty, and the clerk at the desk was an obliging young man with a full head of dark hair, which may have been his own, and an unsuspicious nature. He registered me in a normal manner. I would have signed a phony name if I had thought quickly enough, but he asked for a credit card and I couldn't think of any reason to refuse. Maybe it didn't matter. Solomon had me spotted, and it wouldn't do me any good to run, even if I wanted to. I couldn't escape the long arm of the magician. But it was time I learned the rules of the game if I was going to play—or else I would be the shuttlecock batted from one side of the net to the other.

"Say," I said, turning back to the desk as if on impulse, "have you got a girl registered here? Nice-looking girl with blue eyes and dark hair? Named Ariel?"

"Ariel who?" he asked.

No imagination. I shrugged and put on a sly, man-to-man smile. "Hell, I didn't catch her last name."

He shuffled through the recent cards. "Not today," he said.

"Well," I tried again, "what about a white-haired old boy named Uriel?"

He stopped being so obliging. "Ariel? Uriel? What's the game?"

"Well," I said desperately, "what about a little old lady named Mrs. Peabody?"

But he turned away, his opinion of the human race hardening into the typical desk clerk's cynicism. I was sorry to have been a party to it, but sorrier still that I was no better informed than I was when I started.

I trudged toward the elevator with my room key in my hand. I felt like I was sitting in a poker game and had just discovered that everything was wild except the cards I was holding. I rode the elevator up to the seventh floor. It stopped all right. It didn't keep going up into the stratosphere. The floor was the seventh according to the elevator and the numbers on the doors, and I walked down the hall on the anonymous hotel carpet until I reached room 707. I fumbled the key into the lock and opened the door and stepped into a bottomless black pit through which I went falling, falling, falling . . .

I was spinning, my arms and legs reaching desperately for handholds and footholds in the formless night. I cartwheeled madly through the lightless void, lost and alone and terrified, and I thought to myself that if I could only get out of this eternal dark pit, I would give it all up. I would give up the search for Solomon; I would give up the case; I would give up the agency; I would go back to the classroom; and I would never meddle again in things that didn't concern me, in other people's trouble.

I braced myself for the impact of my body on some unyielding bottom to this pit, but it never came. *This isn't real,* I told myself, but the thought was twisted away from me by a cold, rushing wind. *Illusion!* I screamed, but my voice was lost in the nothingness that enveloped me.

Panic tried to force sound past the tightening muscles of my throat. Tension was growing into rigidity. Soon I would be beyond desperation, beyond saving, and I pushed one sane thought through the gathering block: *If this is illusion, if I am not really falling, if this is a trap like the stairs, then I am standing just inside the door and the light switch is where the light switch always is—to my right against the wall.*

It's a lie, said my reeling senses that knew they were falling. But I hugged the thought to me, and I reached out with my flailing hand where the light switch would be if I were not falling, and—

The lights came on. I was standing just inside the door. I was looking into an ordinary hotel room. A double bed was in front of me flanked by imitation walnut end tables. On the far side of the room, next to a window, was an imitation oak table and two imitation captain's chairs on rollers. A closet was to my right, a bathroom to my left, and I wondered if I was going mad.

I stepped forward and looked back. On the floor was a piece of shiny black glass, about three feet square. I leaned over and dug a finger between the glass and the beige carpet and picked it up. I looked into it.

It wasn't black glass after all. It was a mirror, but it

wasn't silvered. Where the silver should have been, the back was painted a shiny black. My face, square and craggy, looked back at me as if I were staring out of another world, as if that were another person in that world, blank-eyed, ghost-ridden, doomed, and then I realized that the image I saw wasn't all imagination. That was me. Through a glass darkly, yes, but me still, the way I was, the way I felt.

I shuddered and turned the piece of glass over. Scratched in the paint around the edge was an endless string of cabalistic letters, similar to the ones I had noticed on the seal: I felt sure now that they were Hebrew. I pulled the program out of my pocket and compared the two. They were the same letters, but they weren't in the same order. I wished, for the first time in my life, that I could read Hebrew. But this made as much sense as anything else that had happened to me this crazy day.

I walked to the far wall with the square of glass and leaned it carefully against the wall, the mirror face turned away from me. After a few minutes I stopped shaking and walked wearily toward a chair. I slumped into it, letting waves of fatigue sweep up my body from my feet. This was as tired as I could ever remember being, and I hadn't done anything. I must have sat there through the entire program, my body tensed in wait for the terrible and the inexplicable.

I let the day's happenings pass in review inside my puzzled head. Every time disbelief grew too great, I glanced at the black square leaning against the wall.

I was enmeshed in a crazy, fantastic cobwebbery of magic and witchcraft. Nameless, faceless things crouched like obscene spiders in every corner and waited for unwary flies to twitch the web. Gaily, unthinking, unbelieving, I had buzzed in. I was caught. Loops of sticky silk were being wrapped around me until, cocooned, I would lie helplessly awaiting someone's dark pleasure. The only way to save myself was to find out who the spiders were and where they hid. Maybe then they would find that they had a wasp in their web, with a stinger in his tail, who would tear their flimsy strands into worthless pieces and threaten them with death if they tried any funny stuff.

Who was Mrs. Peabody, the little old lady who had drawn me into this deadly game with a crisp, green lure? Was she working against Solomon, or with him? Or was she merely seeking protection? Did Ariel and Uriel have an unknown ally? Was she one of Solomon's own confederates? Was she trying to take his place? Or had it been only a trick by Solomon, safe in his anonymity, to use me against an undetermined third party, or to divert suspicion from himself?

Who was the red witch, Catherine La Voisin, and what plans did she have for me?

Who was Ariel? Who was Uriel? Could I trust them to be as frank and honest as they seemed? What were they, after all, but a witch and a sorcerer? Were they using me? Were they controlling my actions with little twitches of my emotional strings?

But surely I was too unimportant for that. Who cared about me?

And, above all, who was Solomon and what dark deeds did he plan?

If it hadn't been so serious I would have laughed at it as poor melodrama, but melodrama, good or bad, doesn't seem funny when some very nasty possibilities lie in the future.

I was fighting against shadows. I was the blind man in a terminal game of blindman's buff. If I could only tear aside the blinders for a moment and see a face—

What had been the purpose of the black mirror? Had it been another warning? Had it said, more pointedly than words, *Be careful or something really deadly may happen to you*? Or had it been an attempt that failed? That was hard to believe. I didn't know enough to get out of traps.

I'd had enough of traps. I'd had enough of stumbling around in the dark. "More light!" said Goethe. That's what I needed: light. Knowledge. And then I swallowed hard. I had just remembered where Goethe had called for light.

I pulled the bound manuscript out of my pocket, took off my coat and tossed it on the bed, unstrapped my shoulder holster and hung it over the back of the chair, where the butt was within easy reach of my hand, stripped off my tie, and settled back in one of the imitation captain's chairs.

I began leafing through the manuscript, glancing at the headings written in Uriel's neat hand: "Introduction," "Principles," "Equipment," "Simple Spells," "Counter-spells," "Teleportation," "Illusions," "Disguises," "Medical and Other Practical Applications." The last section of the manuscript, ironically, was entitled "Ethics."

I went back to the introduction and began to read carefully. The material had been worked and reworked, simplified, boiled down, and fitted into a theoretical framework. Diverse phenomena had been noted and described, their similarities observed, a reasonable hypothesis derived to explain the phenomena; the hypothesis was used to predict further events, altered, rechecked, and the whole process gone through again and again until the hypothesis was accepted as tentatively proved theory. In other words, a scientific mind had been at work with the aid of the scientific method and out of discredited phenomena had developed a working science.

At least that's what I thought. I couldn't be sure because the manuscript had not been written as a textbook but as an *aide memoire.* Most of the connective and explanatory material that would have made everything much more understandable to me had been omitted. What I held was a notebook filled with personal jottings; they may have been perfectly comprehensible to the author, who could supply the background and examples automatically from memory and experience, but they were only suggestive to the casual reader. And the examples that were apparently present in the manuscript were nothing but headings and mathematical formulations. Sometimes I understood the calculus, but mostly I didn't know what the symbols were supposed to represent.

When mathematicians say that mathematics is the only precise language, they mean when the answer is mathematical, and the inaccuracy of translation begins when you ask them what that answer means in terms of real things. When scientists say, "You can't understand it; you don't have the mathematics," I have the sneaky notion that they don't know what it means in our imperfect world, either.

But my time was not completely wasted on surmises and suspicions. I gathered the general impression that Uriel's theory postulated a store of energy somewhere that ordinarily is unavailable to our world. That store of energy existed in a place which was undefinable except in mathematical terms; the place might be called, inaccurately, "a coexistent universe," parallel with ours but not touching it at any point—or some verbal equivalent that was equally descriptive and equally inexact.

So far the concept was not absurd, not if you matched it against current explanations of the origins of the universe or the behavior of subatomic particles. If you can believe in neutrinos and quarks, you can believe in anything; and the theory of continuous creation of matter must assume some such store of matter or energy.

In any case, there had to be something to Uriel's theory: it worked.

This energy from a coexistent universe, then, was available, sometimes, in certain ways, to people who live in this world. Not by physical means, however: these were limited, by definition, to this place, this moment, this universe. But the mind is unfettered by time and place; it can range anywhere—backward to the beginning of time, forward to the end of the universe, sideways into parallel systems. The mind, properly prepared and properly tuned, can tap that source of energy and channel it into this world to do its will.

In the long and uncertain history of man, through man's effort to control personified forces and spirits, his mind had tapped that source of secret energy, inefficiently, haphazardly. Myths and folklore have recorded the appearances of that energy in the form of gods and demons and fairies and the spirit world and all the other manifestations to which man, in his eternal quest for explanation, has given names. The appearance of the energy was fitful and uncertain because magicians lacked two things: theory and discipline. Where there was no theory, there could be no control, and a wrong theory was worse than no theory at all. And a disciplined mind was seldom found among the warped personalities of priests, witches, and magicians, even though a firm belief in the supernatural or demons or astrology was a necessary ingredient in the process.

What was essential was a scientific mind and an unshakable conviction in the existence of another world, and these two were mutually inconsistent, though perhaps they had not always been. And occasionally, then, desire or fear might accidentally work in the proper manner and call forth what the mind wanted or dreaded most. Because the energy itself was formless. The mind was the matrix and shaped the energy into the thing that it became.

I began to understand why Uriel had objected so violently to the day's programs. The energy could be tapped, but evil minds shaped it to their own desires and called that proof of the presence of evil in the universe. Self-fulfilling prophecy. I returned to the manuscript.

Physical or symbolic devices could help discipline the mind. The symbolic device that worked best was mathematics. Others could be effective, but mathematics expressed relationships exactly without unfortunate connotations or subconscious responses. If you did it properly, you got just what you wanted—no more, no less. And modern developments in mathematics had made possible the conversion of a bastard art into a precise science.

Extramundane energy could be controlled accurately and exactly by use of such mathematical tools as calculus, which took limits; analysis situ—topology—which was concerned with proximity in space, the sort of thing that is involved with telekinesis, for instance; and tensor analysis—absolute differential calculus—which constructed and discussed relations or laws which are generally covariant, which remained valid, that is, when passing from one to another system of coordinates, such as from the coexistent universe to our own. By using the proper equations, the mind could channel the desired amount of energy into the desired function, or bring two or more objects into different relationships. Possibly through this other universe.

I looked up from the manuscript. My mind was boiling like a teakettle. If what I was reading was true—and I had seen it demonstrated in the Crystal Room time after time—then anyone could be a magician. Anyone! It didn't require talent, just belief, knowledge, and determination. I had determination. I could acquire the knowledge. And if I saw the evidence before me, I was enough of a pragmatist to believe.

A metropolitan hotel is a self-contained city. Anything can happen inside its great protective walls—theft, rape, murder, espionage, adultery, conversion, self-sacrifice, saintliness, and conventions of sorcerers. The outside world need never know. But a place like this has its advantages, its own kind of magic. All things are possible, not by use of secret spells and formulae but by the expenditure of strictly mundane energy by hotel employees and strictly U.S. money by guests.

I picked up a device that would have been magical to anyone living before 1876 and asked for room service. And I gave the girl who answered the telephone what was perhaps the oddest order in what must have been a fantastic list of unusual requests.

"I want a book on the history of magic and witchcraft," I said. "Also, see what you can find on higher mathematics, specifically calculus, analysis situ, and tensor analysis. I want them as soon as possible."

"Yes, sir," the girl said. She didn't even ask me to spell anything. "Anything else, sir?"

"A ham sandwich on rye, french fries, and a pot of black coffee," I said.

"Yes, sir," she said. "Is that all, sir?"

"Oh," I said, "and a box of chalk."

Chapter 7

Some mathematicians believe that numbers were invented by human beings, others, equally competent, believe that numbers have an independent existence of their own and are merely observed by sufficiently intelligent mortals.

E. T. Bell, The Magic of Numbers

The first thing I tackled was the ham sandwich. It was a good sandwich, and it didn't suffer from being served under a dull, silvered banquet cover. As I ate it, I leafed through the history of magic, which looked to be the easiest of the lot. Later, after two cups of coffee, I realized that matters were not that simple; the sorts of things one obtains by osmosis from society are often incorrect and always misleading.

The Magus, for instance, was not merely a fancy name for a magician. He had taken his name from that great source of medieval magic, Solomon. Some authorities believed that Solomon's reputation as the greatest of wizards was strictly a later invention; others pointed to the pages devoted to the wisest of all Israelite kings in the Bible, which excite our curiosity without satisfying it. But the Bible is not our only source of information about Solomon; Persian, Arab, and Turkish writers, as well as the Talmudists, passed along legends of his wealth, wisdom, and power. His knowledge made him the most powerful of men, and he commanded all celestial, terrestrial, and infernal spirits; he was obeyed by the subterranean pygmies and gnomes, and by undines, elves, and salamanders.

One author wrote of him, "In his palace paved with crystal Solomon had the jinn and the demons seated at tables of iron, the poor at tables of wood, chiefs of armies at tables of silver, and learned men and doctors of the law at tables of gold. . . . According to the Koran, the jinn worked under his eyes, building palaces and making statues, gardens, ponds, and precious carpets. When he desired to visit distant lands he traveled carried upon their backs."

Solomon's ring was his most valuable possession: by its power he commanded the jinn. But his seal, his mysterious lamp, and his throne also were famous.

The angel Raphael, it was believed, had brought him the ring from God. There was a certain darkness about Solomon's later years, as if he had indeed forsaken the One God of his forefathers and tried to communicate with other, demonic powers. The stories about his magic only grew greater after his death, and by the Middle Ages every alchemist, astrologer, cabalist, and hopeful sorcerer was convinced of Solomon's mastery of the Ancient Art. Somewhere, they thought, all of his intimate possessions still existed, impervious to loss or the deterioration of time because of their magical quality, and they had only to be discovered—the seal, the lamp, the ring, and most of all the book of magic, the Clavicule—and the aspirant magician himself could command demons and be as wise, as rich, and most of all as powerful as the fabled king. The great search for his secrets never slackened until the belief in magic dwindled away under the materialism of the Industrial Revolution.

The most important artifact to be discovered was the so-called Key of Solomon. Many versions circulated throughout Europe, all purporting to be the one and only Clavicule, written in Solomon's own hand. The manuscript contained detailed descriptions of the preparations and ceremony for summoning demons—and, perhaps more important, for dismissing them. The instructions were so detailed and so difficult to follow exactly, as well as having possibly symbolic or cryptic meanings, that the magicians could not succeed. But they also could try until they died of senile decay without losing hope or losing faith in "Solomon."

It must have been a great period for con artists, I thought.

Christianity brought other, darker elements into the search for magical power. What began as a search for knowledge not unlike the modern scientific search became a heretical belief in other powers than God; magic became a perversion practiced in private, a dedication to evil, witchcraft. The summoning of demons became a pact with Satan accompanied by all sorts of nasty rites and submissions.

Ariel and Uriel, like Gabriel, were the names of angels. It was a relief to discover whose side I was on. Catherine La Voisin, on the other hand, was a professional palmist and clairvoyant during the reign of Louis XIV. She secretly sold love charms and death spells to her more desperate clients. Besides being a witch, she was a poisoner and was involved in several lewd, bloody Amatory Masses said over the naked body of Madame de Montespan, Louis XIV's mistress, after the King had deserted her for the Duchess de la Vallière. But the Masses, which involved, some reports said, cutting the throats of children, were not effective. Finally, after a death Mass said against Louis by his now maddened former mistress succeeded no better than the love spells, a plot was made to poison the King, La Voisin was arrested, convicted, and burned alive.

What kind of person, I wondered, would take the name of someone like that? I was sure now that I wanted nothing at all to do with her modern namesake.

Terms swirled like bats' wings through my head: Amatory Masses, Black Masses, Mortuary Masses, Masses in the cold, cold ground; Cabalas and Schemhamphoras; covens and Sabbaths and dark rites; obscene ceremonies and violent trials. The witches were bad enough, but it almost seemed as if the witch hunters were worse. Anything was permissible in the conviction of an accused witch. The *Malleus Maleficarium* of Heinrich Kramer and James Sprenger, the famed Hammer of Witches, recommended the following tactics to the ecclesiastical judge: "While the officers are preparing for the questioning, let the accused be stripped. . . . And the reason for this is that they should search for any instruments of witchcraft sewn into her clothes; for they often make such instruments, at the instruction of devils, out of the limbs of unbaptized children, the purpose being that those children should be deprived of the beatific vision. . . . If she will not confess the truth voluntarily, let him order the officers to bind her with cords, and apply her to some engine of torture. . . . Then let her be released again at someone's earnest request, and taken on one side, and let her again be persuaded; and in persuading her, let her be told that she can escape the death penalty. . . ."

I turned with relief to the sanity of mathematics. I plowed my way through differential and integral calculus, and as they came back to me Uriel's formulae became a little more meaningful. With a briefer perusal of the elements of analysis situ and tensor analysis, I surrendered to a feeling of mastery. It may have been illusory, but it felt good after the confusions of the day.

If Uriel's manuscript was what it pretended to be, if what he said he had discovered was true, I now was qualified to work magic. I hesitated, remembering the Sorcerer's Apprentice, seeing Mickey Mouse in my memory racing back and forth with buckets, trying to undo his careless mistakes. But I also remembered Ariel, who was depending on me, and Solomon, who was waiting for me to stumble into his ungentle hands, and I decided to give it a try.

Where should I start? I remembered the casual way in which one of the speakers had summoned a cold drink. I thought about a nice cold mint julep or a Tom Collins, but unthought about them just as quickly. I shouldn't try anything complicated while I was still learning. I settled for something simple: an ordinary highball. Bourbon and soda. That shouldn't be difficult.

I leafed through Uriel's manuscript until I came to the section headed "Simple Spells." I went over it once quickly and then read it over again more carefully, taking notes. Okay. I turned to "Equipment." The only essential piece of equipment, the manuscript said, was a piece of chalk, or even pencil and paper, and these were only aids to concentration in jotting down equations. Someone who had an excellent memory or was brilliant in mathematics eventually might be able to keep the equations in his head, but I had neither memory nor brilliance. I took a piece of chalk out of the box and held it tightly in my sweaty hand.

It is also helpful, the manuscript suggested, to include an element of similarity in the spell if the mind is not accustomed to thinking in mathematical terms. That described me, all right, I thought, and got a water glass from the bathroom, dribbled a few drops of water into the bottom, and placed it in front of me on the table. Beside the glass I chalked a small circle and jotted down the recommended equation. Nothing happened.

Would it work? I stopped myself from thinking in that direction. Without belief the mind cannot function properly. It did work. There was no doubt of that. I had seen it work. I could make it work.

I said the equation aloud, linking the unknowns to the object I wanted and the place I wanted it. Nothing happened.

"In the beginning," the manuscript said, "verbal equivalents are often helpful."

Verbal equivalents. I felt foolish doing it, but I shrugged and chanted, "Highball, highball, come to me, come to Casey Kingman, the private eye from Kansas City, Kansas, who is presently located in room seven oh seven of—"

Suddenly there was a glass in the circle. The instant before the circle had been empty. Now the glass was there. Amber. Miraculous. I stared at it, wide-eyed and unbelieving. I had done it. I had worked magic—or maybe, if Uriel was right, I had practiced a new science.

I reached a trembling hand toward the glass and picked it up. I raised it to my lips and sipped gingerly, letting it roll back over my tongue. Phew-w-w! The liquid sprayed over the brocade curtains as it flew from my mouth. The bourbon was lousy. The soda was water. And the water was hot.

I put the glass down feeling chastened and properly humble. Obviously I was not yet an adept. I was lucky, perhaps, that I had not summoned a barrel, or a vat, or the spirit of the vine, himself, Bacchus and the bacchantes, to tear me to pieces. Like Prospero I felt like forswearing magic for all time. It was too dangerous for a man like me; I'd take my chances with easier tools like guns and knives.

But I couldn't give up. Too much depended on my success, not least my life.

I paced the floor restlessly. Damn it! I needed help. The speaker on spells had summoned not only a glass but a girl. Or teleported her, I caught myself. It was easy to fall into Solomon's trap of describing these phenomena in terms of magic instead of science.

I needed somebody to talk to, somebody to answer my questions, somebody to teach me. Neither Ariel nor Uriel were registered under those names in the hotel. I didn't know where they were, what rooms they were in, whether they were staying in the hotel at all. I had no way of getting in contact with either one of them. I had to wait until they wanted to talk to me. Or did I?

I needed a link, something connected with one of them. I hadn't even met Uriel. I might as well cross him off immediately. What of Ariel? I thought about her for a moment, smiled, and then pulled myself out of my reverie. She had handled the program. I discarded that link quickly.

A number of other persons had handled the program as well, some of them perhaps more intimately, and I had no desire to confront an irate printer.

I looked around the room and noticed my jacket lying on the bed. Of course. Girls always leave hairs on coats. Sometimes makeup, too. But always hairs.

I picked up the coat. There were hairs. Some of them were short and blond; they were mine. One was long and red. I rolled it into a ball between my fingers and was about to throw it away when I had a second thought. I straightened it carefully, slipped it into a hotel envelope, and put the envelope in my inside coat pocket. I patted it. I had La Voisin in there, and it felt good. I fought back the feeling; power was not my aim. Finally I found a hair that was dark and about the right length.

I held it thoughtfully. After a few moments I raised it to my nose, but it had no odor. It looked like Ariel's, but was I sure? Could I do a better job this time? Was there any danger to Ariel if I muffed it again? I decided that there wasn't; if there was any danger, she would have protected herself against it. Otherwise, what was the use of being a witch? The worst that could happen, I decided, would be the summoning of some other girl, Catherine La Voisin, for instance. I shivered. The worst was bad enough.

This time my preparations were more thorough. I got a cake of soap from the bathroom and started to work on it with my penknife. I'm no artist, but soap is a forgiving material and in just a few minutes I had a surprisingly good model of a reclining nude. It didn't look like Ariel, of course, but I had an answer for that. I moistened the top of the figure's head, coiled the hair by drawing it between thumbnail and fingernail, and stuck the hair to the damp soap.

I sat at the table going over the section in the manuscript labeled "Teleportation" until I thought I knew it by heart. I knelt on the floor and drew a chalk circle on the floor, placed the figurine inside the circle, and chalked an analysis situ equation around it.

I stood up and compared what I had done with the instructions. Everything checked. "*X* is for Ariel," I muttered. "*Y* is the circled spot in this room." I recited the equation aloud, trying to concentrate not only on the equation but on the identities involved. I closed my eyes, the way I always used to do when I wanted to focus on something I had to learn. "Wherever you are, Ariel, come to me. Come to this spot. Appear in this circle. Ariel, come to me. . . ."

Air fanned my face. I opened my eyes. Standing in the circle was a pair of small, bare white feet. I heard a gasp. My eyes traveled up a pair of shapely legs and then to a face I knew. It was Ariel, all right. All of her and not much more besides. Her eyes were wide and blue and startled. My eyes, no doubt, were startled, too, because it was obvious that Ariel had just stepped out of a bath or shower.

The "not much more" was a towel which she had draped hastily in front of her. She let out her breath. It sounded like relief, but it might have been anger. I sank back into the chair, speechless and suddenly weak but oddly satisfied that my earlier impressions of her figure had been vindicated in a way that I would never have thought of, and sooner than I could have imagined.

I thought about a gust of air, and the wind whistled past

my head and tried to whip the towel aside. Ariel clutched at it with both hands, frowning, looking annoyed. But her annoyance was sabotaged by a wispy smile that tried to turn up the corners of her mouth. It was a nice mouth, and I wished I could make it smile more broadly. "That's very naughty," she said.

And she stooped gracefully, as if she had practiced the delicate maneuver with the towel for hours, picked up the soap figurine, muttered a few words, and disappeared, towel, figurine, and all.

I found my voice after it was too late. "Ariel, Ariel," I called after her. "Where can I find you? Where—?"

But it was no use. My words vanished. She was gone. The circle was empty. And with her she had taken my last hope of getting the answers I needed.

I felt a little better about myself and the magic business, but I wasn't proud of the way I reacted to opportunity. Now I would have to wait until tomorrow to accomplish anything. And tomorrow might be too late. Who knew what dark things waited for me in the night?

Fifteen minutes later I remembered the handkerchief. I pulled it out of my pocket, remembering how it had wiped away her tears as we sat on the stairs that led nowhere. But I found myself staring at orange smears. All my ventures into magic had been bungled, one way or another. It would be just my luck to summon the carnivorous Catherine La Voisin, complete with mammary glands, Amatory Masses, and poison.

But I had summoned Ariel once, I told myself with growing determination. I could do it again. I could. I knew I could.

The circle and the equation still were chalked on the floor. They had worked before. I saw no reason they wouldn't serve a second time. Perhaps they even retained some residual connection. I dropped the handkerchief in the center of the circle, took the glass of water that still remained on the desk beside the aborted highball, and sprinkled the handkerchief with water from my fingertips.

"Ariel, Ariel," I said, "by the tears you shed into this handkerchief, come now to claim it, come here to me to claim your tears again. . . ."

This time I was not surprised when Ariel appeared within the circle. I blinked and she was there. That was the way it seemed to work in the magic world; things either were or weren't—there was nothing in between, no fading in or out. It was a completely black and white system; like a computer switch, it was either on or off. I decided to think about it like that—as if it was a computer. Maybe it would help my results.

What I was surprised about was Ariel's attire. She was more modestly clad in a nightgown—but not much. Her hair was brushed and shiny around her shoulders, and her black gown was lacy and revealing. I took a deep, quick breath. Perfume. She was very desirable to me at that moment. Almost beautiful.

But I was bothered by a couple of questions. The nightgown appeared impractical for everyday use, and I didn't think that most girls put on perfume when they went to bed alone. Then I chided myself for my suspicions.

Ariel put on a frown. "I don't know how you've become adept so quickly, Gabriel, but this sort of thing has got to stop. It's disconcerting, to say the least, being whisked around constantly, not knowing whether you will be here or there the next moment. Besides, what will people say? What about my uncle? What about the house detective?"

I had to laugh. I couldn't help it. There was witchcraft in the Crystal Room, possession and werewolves, magic and murder, and the nice witch in the black lace nightgown was worried about house detectives and indiscretion.

Her frown twisted as she tried to keep a straight face, and then she was laughing, too. It was the kind of magical moment one wishes would never stop, and then I noticed that she was looking down at her feet. My laughter died, and I jumped to my feet.

"Wait!" I said. "Don't go away! I've got to talk to you! There are questions you have to answer for me!"

"Well," she said, "I'm not going to talk while I'm standing in the middle of the room. Let me out."

"Let you out?" I repeated blankly.

She pointed down at her feet, stamping one impatiently. "The circle," she said. "Don't you know anything? I can't get out until it's broken."

I rubbed out a chalked arc with the sole of my shoe, and she brushed past me in a delicate cloud of black lace and fragrance. I breathed deeply and turned toward her, but she was looking back toward the circle, her eyes on the handkerchief with which I had summoned her. Before she could move, I leaned over, picked up the handkerchief, and started to stuff it into my pocket.

She held out her hand, snapping her fingers meaningfully, the way a person might do to a dog who has brought back the thrown stick but now is reluctant to release it. I resented it, but guilt made me pull out the square of linen and hand it to her. I looked away as she spread the handkerchief flat and stared at the orange smears. She frowned for a moment and then her face melted into tears.

"Oh," she wailed, turning blindly toward the bed. "You've been with that redheaded witch, kissing her, making love to her! You've deserted and gone over to their side!" She fell on the bed, sobbing. I couldn't tell whether it was rage or sorrow.

"But—but—" I tried to get out. "I can explain it. I didn't do anything. I didn't have anything to do with it, as a matter of fact. She backed me into a corner and—"

"Oh, it's always the woman," she got out between sobs. "The man's never to blame," she added, inconsistently. And then to compound the confusion, she said, "If you could only see that poisonous vampire as she really is, you wouldn't get within ten feet of her."

I sat down on the edge of the bed and patted her shaking shoulder. It was a nice shoulder, and I liked patting it. I would have liked to pat something else, but I decided to be content with a shoulder.

"I wouldn't get within ten feet of her anyway," I said, shuddering. "Once is too much. Besides, she isn't my type."

She moved her shoulder away from my hand. "Don't touch me," she said savagely. And then she added, more softly, "What *is* your type?"

I thought about it. As the words came out they were as much a revelation to me as they were to her. "A girl with dark hair," I said, "and blue eyes, not too tall, about your size and shape—"

She sat up, brushing away her tears with the back of her hand, like any urchin. If I could have kept my eyes off the nightgown and kept from remembering what the towel had failed to conceal, I would have thought she looked like a little girl. But there was no chance of that kind of mistake.

Her eyes were bright and blue, suddenly undimmed by tears. "Really?"

I nodded. "You bet!" I said.

There must have been conviction in my voice. She smiled. "Did she really back you into a corner?"

"So help me Hermes!" I said. Hermes Trismegistus, the legendary Egyptian founder of magic, was a name I had run across in my research; his legendary Emerald Tablets were reputed to be even more effective than the Key of Solomon, and his followers among magicians were known as hermetic philosophers. Ariel looked impressed by my learning. "Tell me. What's happened since the session this afternoon? What is Uriel going to do?"

"He has decided to stay and fight. He's going to help in any way he can. He swore to me that he would strip Solomon of his powers. 'I created this monster,' he said, 'and I will destroy it.' The werewolf and the little girl were terrible mistakes. For Solomon, that is. The greatest danger the magician runs is pride; he must continually be humble or, like Doctor Faustus, he is lost."

Now it was my turn to be impressed. Doctor Faustus, indeed! "I don't quite understand," I said.

"If that attempt to kill Uriel hadn't been so obvious," she explained patiently, "or if the mistreatment of the young man and the little girl had not been so gross, I don't think Uriel would ever have done anything about the situation. You've got to understand and not expect too much of him. He's just a mild little man who wouldn't hurt anything.

When he saw trouble heading his way, he always went around the block to avoid it. As long as he could convince himself that things weren't too bad, he was willing to let them go along any way they would. All he wants to do is to continue his research and let other people use it as they will. But now he's made up his mind."

"Uriel?" I said dubiously.

"He's the best of the lot," Ariel said. "None of the others can touch him."

"Not even Solomon?"

"Not even Solomon," she said positively.

"Nevertheless," I said, "there's just the two of you? You and Uriel? That's all?"

She nodded.

"Tough odds," I said slowly.

"And Uriel's not well," she said. "He scoffs at the idea of the Mass of St. Secaire. 'Superstition!' he says. But he knows that he could do something similar if he wanted to. But he couldn't. He couldn't bring himself to use the Art for evil purposes, and in his heart he can't believe that anyone else would either. So he's tried to protect himself with counter-spells but they're weakened by lack of conviction."

"Well," I said, "now there's three of us."

I was rewarded with a glance of pure gratitude. It was enough for any man. "Thank you—Gabriel," she said. "But what about you? Did you—did you have any luck finding out Solomon's name?"

I shook my head regretfully. "All I found was this," I said. I pulled the airline ticket out of my coat pocket. "And I don't have any real reason to believe that it was Solomon's."

She took the ticket, felt it, smelled it, looked it over

carefully, and handed it back. "It feels right. There's an aura of residual psychic force, but it doesn't have to be Solomon's. But it feels right. In any case, keep it! I don't know what good it will do, but it might fit in with something else."

Suddenly she stiffened and was still. I looked at her. She was staring at something across the room, like a cat looking at creatures no one else can see. But when I turned I saw that she was looking at the back of the mirror I had leaned against the wall.

I walked to the wall and started to turn the mirror around so that she could look at it. "I stepped on it when I came into the room. It gave me the oddest feeling."

She gave me a sharp glance. "I'll bet it did," she said. And then before I could turn the mirror more than halfway, "Careful! That's enough! I've heard of black mirrors, but I never saw one. Someone wants to get rid of you."

"Oh," I said, and shrugged. "I imagine it was just another warning. The sensation stopped as soon as I turned on the light."

"Don't believe it," she said, her voice shaky. "You were either very strong or very lucky. In the black mirror, time and space are meaningless. A few seconds is like an eternity. You could have gone mad. Or some say that if the mirror is broken while you're trapped, you'll die. Or just disappear, trapped in that dark world forever. And that may be worse."

I shivered. I was doing a lot of that lately, and I thought, I should have worn a sweater. Or my shockproof persona. This was not my kind of danger. I could have faced a dozen bullets and not felt half so cold.

"But how did they work it?" she went on, frowning. "Do

they know your name?" I shook my head. Ariel snapped her fingers. "That witch, La Voisin! When she kissed you, did she run her fingers through your hair?"

"Why, yes," I said slowly. "Come to think of it. I guess she did. So what?"

"You poor unsuspecting males," she said, shaking her head in sorrow for the whole other sex. "Did you think she was overcome with desire for you?"

"Well," I said, a bit offended, "as a matter of fact—" But she was up and coming toward me. I watched her warily.

"This is what she did," Ariel said and put her face up and raised her arms and pulled my head down to hers. Our lips met. There was nothing electric about it, I'll have to confess that, but it was sweet and satisfying. Maybe better than electricity. I felt my pulse begin to pound. Her hand moved tenderly up the back of my neck into my hair. "M-m-m," she said, her lips half-parted.

Finally she pulled away, her eyes glazed and distant. Then, as my eyes focused again, I saw her eyes snap back to the here and now. "Oh, dear," she said. She held out her hand to me. "Look!"

I looked. Several of my blond hairs had come away in her hand. I winced. The redheaded witch had something that belonged to me, that gave her power over me. God knew what she was going to do with it. If she hadn't already done it. Then I thought of something. "We came out even, then," I said. "I have one of hers."

Her eyes narrowed and her other hand reached out. "Let me have it!" she said eagerly.

I got the envelope from my coat and handed it to her. With the envelope held tightly in her left hand, she stooped and picked up the piece of chalk where I had left it on the floor. She stepped into the circle on the rug, bent and replaced the arc I had rubbed out with my shoe, and disappeared.

"Hey," I yelled. "Wait! I still don't know where to find you—"

That's me. Always too late.

Chapter 8

Underneath all the tales there does lie something different from the tales. How different? In this—that the thing which is invoked is a thing of a different nature, however it may put on a human appearance or indulge in its servants their human appetites. It is cold, it is hungry, it is violent, it is illusory. The warm blood of children and the intercourse at the Sabbath do not satisfy it. It wants something more and other; it wants "obedience," it wants "souls," and yet it pines for matter. It never was, and yet it always is.

Charles Williams, Witchcraft

I'm not much of a dreamer. Oh, I dream like everybody else, but as dreams they're pretty ordinary: dread of being late for a class, libidinous longings for some girl or other of the moment or of the distant past, fear of some unseen menace or of something terrible about to happen . . . nothing that would interest a discriminating psychoanalyst. Nothing lavish and multicolored and meaningful.

But my recent experiences must have programmed my unconscious for a real Sandman Production. Not much after I had gone to sleep, as I calculated time in my dreaming condition, I found myself high above an evening landscape, looking down upon a scene that seemed strangely antique. A countryside was below, a farming community it seemed, but the fields were small as if they were intended for tilling by a man and an animal, or a man alone, and the fields were separated by rows of small, gnarled trees. Next to each small field, black now with the crops all gathered in for the year, was a small cottage with a thatched roof. They, in turn, were clustered around a more stately house with more extensive grounds, virtually a mansion, I supposed.

Unlike most dreams, which tend to be blurred around the edges, often in black and white, and seldom with more than one sensory stimulus besides sight, in this dream everything was sharply focused and touched the full sensorium. The air that rushed through my nose and into my lungs was crisp and cold and clean, uncontaminated by pollutants other than wood smoke curling from fireplaces below. I knew how the straw felt on the thatched roofs of the cottages and the packed dirt that formed the floors, and I could hear the tolling of bells from the steeple of a village church, whether to sound the hour or to call to worship I did not know.

And I had senses I had never possessed in real life: I could look down through the roofs of the houses at the people in them. In most of the cottages the inhabitants already were asleep although night was not yet complete, but in a few of the one-room dwellings people were still awake and active. Most of them were women, and they were naked or disrobing, as if on some common signal—perhaps the bell?—but not for bed.

"They have a spot on their body which feels no pain, but when it tingles they know they are summoned." The voice came from behind me, but I could not turn my head to see who had spoken.

I continued to stare below, unable, really, to look away. Most of the women were old or middle-aged, and their bodies were hardly the kind to fill a young man's dreams. They were leathery and stringy and ill-favored, as if life had not been kind to them. But a few were young and reasonably attractive, though somewhat thick-waisted and heavy-thighed by contemporary standards. Rubens would have enjoyed them. One of them, however, looked like the girl next door, if you were lucky about places to live; she was slender and high-breasted and, well, virginal—sort of untouched looking and a little tremulous, too, as if whatever she was doing she had never done before and wasn't too sure it wasn't a terrible mistake and she should back out while she still could.

To tell the truth, she looked a lot like Ariel, and I felt a twinge of envy toward the old woman who was smearing the girl's body with some sort of lotion or salve. There was a lot of that going on in the cottages, women being rubbed down by others or doing it to themselves. Even in the mansion, I saw now, the same sort of thing was happening. In a bedroom decorated with silk wall hangings and a canopy bed and a thick rug, a dark-haired woman was standing naked in front of a fire. An older woman was anointing her, and she was preening herself in front of a mirror, clearly admiring her aristocratic figure. I admired it, too, and felt a bit sheepish about it, as if I were a voyeur, but then I told myself that it was only a dream, and a man should be able to enjoy his own dreams without guilt.

A larger group was gathered in one of the cottages. An ugly, middle-aged man was sitting on a stool reading from a book. He had a turban on his head and a bat was perched on the turban, and his eyes were demonic.

"That's a sorcerer, you know," said the voice behind me,

"and he's reading from a Black Book." The voice said it that way, in capitals, and I figured it was talking about a Grimoire, one of the books of magic I had seen advertised in the program that day. But I still couldn't turn my head to see who was speaking.

A skull and a bone were placed inside a circle near the hearth, and cabalistic signs were traced in and around the circle into the dirt floor. A caldron boiled over the fire in the fireplace. It was filled with toads and snakes and other vile substances, as well as with what seemed to be the body of a baby. I felt a touch of horror at the thought, as if what had started as a harmless show had turned into something ugly and perhaps worse.

On the mantel was a burning candle and beside it a mummified hand whose fingertips had been lit. "A hand of glory," the voice said behind me. From the caldron women were dipping some of the fluid. It was this they were rubbing on their naked bodies or on the bodies of their companions.

I could smell the fluid mixed with the old sweat of a life of hard labor—they almost never bathed—and it was nauseating.

"The magic unguent contains aconite and belladonna as well as hellebore root and hemlock," said the voice behind me. "That's enough to give anyone strange sensations, maybe even delusions—such as being able to fly through the air to some forbidden meeting."

As I watched, the naked women one by one got astride broomsticks and vanished up the fireplace. They emerged from the chimney and sailed into the night sky like every version of Halloween that has been commercialized and denatured in our time; only here it wasn't funny or pleasantly eerie; it was frightening.

The beautiful witch in the cottage and the beautiful witch in the mansion disappeared in the same way. It didn't matter that fires were blazing in the fireplaces or that the chimneys were too small. But that's how it is in dreams: a different kind of logic prevails. Maybe that was true, as well, when people believed in witches.

The strangest part of their departure, however, was that they rode their broomsticks the wrong way, with the straw in front of them and a lighted candle stuck in the straw as if to light their way through the darkness to their darker destination. And once they were in the air it seemed as if some of them were not alone on their brooms, as if something else, monstrous and misshapen, rode behind them, an arm—or something like an arm—familiarly wrapped around a waist.

Perhaps that wasn't the strangest part after all. I suddenly discovered that the reason I could look down on this scene from above was that I was high in the air myself. I, too, was astride a broomstick. I was naked, and my whole body tingled with open nerve endings, but I wasn't cold. A chill of another kind prickled my skin, however, as I saw that a scaly arm was around my waist, a sharp chin pressed into my shoulder, and I smelled something foul and alien. I forced myself to look behind me.

A hideous face leered at me. The expression of a vicious murderer had been impressed upon the basic features of a toad, and when it smiled, as it did now, the lips parted from warty ear to warty ear, exposing sharp, mottled teeth.

"Ready?" it said.

"Ready for what?" I asked, although I didn't really want to know. I wanted to get out of there, to wake up, but I couldn't do either one.

"For the Sabbath," it said. And without waiting for an answer it tugged at the broom and we set off through the night sky at a speed which blew my hair straight back from my head, although the candle set in the straw in front of me did not flicker.

"Where are we going?" I shouted into the slipstream, but the demon behind me—I was sure it was a demon—didn't answer. When I forced myself to look at it again, it grinned broadly at me. The teeth looked as if they could tear me apart in a couple of quick bites.

I didn't look back again. Some fates are better if you don't look them in the face. I tugged at the arm around my waist. It was rough and scaly and incredibly strong, or I had grown weak, because I could not budge it. I would have thrown myself off the broom and trusted myself to the possibilities of surviving a long fall. In dreams, I told myself, people always wake up before they reach the ground. Of course that may be because we only hear from those who don't hit the ground.

Still, I would have taken my chances.

The trip seemed to continue interminably, but also to be almost instantaneous. Dreams don't worry about inconsistency.

Finally the demon spoke again in my ear. "There!"

I looked down. Below was a flattened mountain top. A gigantic fire blazed in the middle of a kind of clearing. Strange shadows danced and cavorted obscenely around it. Then stick figures like children's drawings swooped down from the sky, naked witches and sorcerers and demons on broomsticks descending from the night sky like falling leaves to stop upon that blasted mountain.

I wondered about the people who lived nearby. Well, perhaps there wasn't anybody in the forest—a hunter or two, a wood gatherer. What did they think about these strange happenings? And then I thought, Of course! That's how the stories about witches' Sabbaths got started. And then I thought, But this is only a dream. But why should I dream of a mountain top like this and naked witches and broomsticks with the straw the wrong side to? And why did this dream go on and on in a linear fashion? Dreams were jumbled and broken. Weren't they?

"Brocken!" the demon said.

Brocken. Yes, that was where I got the mountain top. This was the legendary location of the witches' Sabbath. Brocken. In the Harz Mountains, in the Black Forest, one of the wildest and most savage areas of northern Germany. I remembered reading about it. Here was where Goethe placed the witches' Sabbath in *Faust.* I remembered a map in which even the cartographer had paid tribute to the legend with images of witches on broomsticks flying above the mountain.

But then I had time for no more soothing explanations of my dream state. My broomstick swooped down out of the sky toward the mountain top like a dive bomber coming in on its target. Just before we hit the ground, the demon—a hot pilot, all right, and a smartass—pulled up on the stick. The broomstick braked like a jet reversing its thrust and settled gently the last half-foot. My feet, knees stiff, met the ground. The broomstick dropped to the rocks beneath. I was left standing, trembling and uncertain, before a scene of unspeakable abandon.

I swallowed hard to get the lump out of my throat. "Good landing," I said sarcastically.

In one part of the clearing a group of naked women were dancing wildly in a circle, facing outward, hands clasped each to the next. Some were young and attractive, some were old and sharp-featured, but all of them were alike in their possession by some demonic fury that drove them to incredible feats of contortion and endurance.

"It may be novel," I said, "but it will never bring back vaudeville."

In another area a group of women and demons were seated alternately around a big stone table. The women were unlovely and didn't know the appearance of soap, but the demons were worse. They were like ill-assorted pieces of men and animals stuck together by a whimsical blind butcher; each was different and each was uglier than the next. On the table was a bowl of meat that resembled the parts of an infant. They were passing favorite pieces to each other, demon tempting witch and witch, demon, until, satiated, they rose from the table and joined another dance around a peculiarly deformed tree. The demons faced toward the tree and the naked witches faced away from it, and they threw their bodies about obscenely.

"When do things get started around here?" I asked.

"Soon enough," the demon behind me said grumpily.

In the center of the clearing a fire leaped and soared into the night. Rather than pushing back the darkness, it, too, seemed in a kind of dance with the blackness, with fingers of flame interlaced with the night. The fire seemed to be fed not by logs but by a jet of gas from deep in the mountain; from time to time I could catch a whiff of rotten eggs, sulfur, and hydrogen sulfide.

"Brimstone," said the voice behind me.

On the far side of the fire, only occasionally revealed by it, were three big stone chairs, almost like thrones. Three people were sitting in them, but I couldn't see who they were because of the flames.

"Some people at a party just never get into the spirit of things," I said, but as I said it a hand pushed me hard in the back, and I plunged toward the fire.

I dodged to one side and even so felt the heat scorch my face. The hand pushed me again. I tried to turn to confront my tormentor, my own personal demon, but each time the hand or claw pushed me again. When I looked up I found myself standing in front of the stone chairs, naked, but more than that feeling terribly exposed and vulnerable but unwilling to appear self-conscious by trying to cover myself. Because I was standing in front of a Presence.

In the central throne, as I thought of it now, sat a creature who was as dark as sin but whose very blackness seemed to radiate an aura, as if darkness could blaze. This creature, too, was part man and part animal, but more care had been taken with his construction, as if the demons were botched attempts at creating what sat upon the throne. Perhaps half human and one-quarter animal, the other quarter was something supernatural from which it derived its *authority*.

Three long, curly horns rose from a narrow, dark-polled head, two ordinary horns and one between them that was luminous like a firefly's tail. The eyes seemed human for a moment, and then I noticed that the yellow pupil in the dark iris was a vertical slit like the eye of a cat. The face was that of a goatlike man. The body seemed manlike down to the waist, although it was covered with black hair almost like fur, but the lower regions were animal, with the hips of a quadruped and the hooves and narrow legs of a goat. Its shoulders looked strangely humped, as if it had been wearing an opera cloak and the cloak had slipped off to rest against the back of the throne.

I could believe that it was a fallen angel towering above me, who had taken on the semblance of a man to mock humanity and the attributes of an animal to illustrate man's beastliness. But I preferred to think of it as a teratology, the monstrous result of a mating between animal and human that now sought its revenge for the hate it had experienced by forcing humans to become animals in front of it.

"You could make a fortune in a sideshow," I said bravely, but my voice broke and betrayed me.

Then it spoke, ignoring me, and I knew it was both male and supernatural. "A new convert?" he said. His voice rumbled like thunder beyond the hills, as if he held in reserve a great power that he could wield if necessary.

"I'm an atheist," I said.

"So much the better."

"I don't believe in you either."

He laughed and then his goat's face grew serious. "You must be mistaken. Why are you here on this sacred ground if you are not of our faith?"

"I don't know why I'm here," I said, "but I think it's the result of too much new information absorbed too quickly.

This is only a dream, you know, and you are only a figment of my imagination."

Satan laughed again. The thunder was now this side of the hills, and it was threatening and lewd. It did my nerves no good, and I told myself that I would have to take all this up with a psychiatrist the first chance I had. "A figment, am I?" he bellowed. "A nightmare, is it?" He waved a scaly hand at all the wanton, sickening activity going on around us. "Tell me that you don't find all this worshipful behavior seductive! Tell me that you don't itch to join in the celebration of the Sabbath!"

"Obviously," I said, "all this comes out of the depths of my subconscious, and therefore it must—I must—" I lost the remark somewhere because I had noticed that his left hand had come to rest on the person who occupied the lesser throne on that side. The person was the naked woman I had seen in the mansion, the proud aristocrat who now seemed just as proud to sit at the left hand of the Devil. That hand was doing something lewd and disgusting to her, and she seemed to enjoy it.

On the right—"That's the less favored spot," said the demon behind me—sat the village maiden who looked like Ariel and suffered in a seeming paralysis of terror the indignities offered by Satan's right hand.

"You cannot deny it," Satan said. "You would like to be where I am now, handling these creatures as I do, everyone in this congregation eager to do me the slightest service, overjoyed to degrade themselves at my whim, panting for my smile, lusting for my touch, coveting the pain and humiliation I may choose to inflict upon them. Who would not want to be me?"

"None of us is perfect," I said.

"You make a joke to hold back terror," he said, "telling yourself that this is only a dream, that you will wake up. But what is nightmare and what is reality? Can you trust your senses any more? What is real and what is impossible? Can you tell them apart?"

I had no answer to that. He had struck me in a vulnerable spot. Within the past twenty-four hours I had seen too many things happen that I would have sworn were impossible. Perhaps this wasn't a dream. But it had to be. I had to be asleep and dreaming. It made no sense otherwise. How else could I find myself back in the Dark Ages, at a witches' Sabbath, among those who believed that these things were real, Satan and his powers? How else could I see the demons as they had imagined them, as they could not possibly have existed? How else could I find myself going through the rituals they thought were a way to power over the things of this earth?

"You will see how real it is," Satan said, and rose from his chair. He towered above me. The rock platform on which his throne rested gave him an advantage of a foot or so, but he was big. He seemed to me to stand more than seven feet tall, with huge, muscular shoulders and arms and slender, goatlike legs. Standing, he was indisputably male, though not humanly male; his maleness, erect and gigantic, was scaly and rough.

As he stood, giant leathery wings unfolded behind him and spread like darkness over the scene. The fire leaped high behind me, reddening Satan's body. "Come!" he thundered. "Do me homage!"

The demons and the witches and the sorcerers rushed to be first in line to bow before his Satanic majesty, and as he turned and bent over to expose his backside to his worshipers he looked over his shoulder to leer at me. The aristocratic lady was first in line to kiss one hairy buttock with apparent adoration. It was not as clean as the backsides of most goats, I thought, but his followers were undeterred.

"He has a second face there, you know," the demon behind me said, but it looked like only a filthy buttock to me.

"I'm not sure I'd like the face any better," I said.

When Satan tired of this game, he turned, spilling his worshipers to one side, careless of who might be injured, and spread his wings again. "You will renounce your faith in God the uncaring, God the remote, and you will affirm your faith in me, who is here, who hears your prayers and answers them, who reigns on earth!"

A group of demons came from the darkness beyond the fire carrying a large cross fashioned roughly of wood, a cross such as might have been used to crucify a man. The witches and demons and sorcerers moved forward to dance and spit and evacuate upon the cross while they praised the power and the beauty of Satan.

"Our father who wert in heaven," they said. And "Satan is now and shall forever be our Lord, the king of all things here on earth. To Satan we swear eternal loyalty. In all things we are his, yea to the grave and beyond."

Satan, standing there majestically, his arms folded across his massive chest, accepted their homage. The frenzy of his worshipers grew into mania. They lifted the cross they had defiled and cast it into the flames. It stood upside down and blazed with an infernal light.

"I prefer a less formal service," I said.

I felt something hot and sharp pressed against my back. I twitched, but I was not going to surrender myself to the game.

"We shall conclude our service," Satan said, "with the customary orgy." He turned to the aristocratic lady standing beside him and enfolded her body, shuddering with ecstasy and pain, within his arms and then within the cloak of his wings. The brutality with which he took her was as repulsively erotic as sadism. The rest of the witches and sorcerers and demons immediately fell upon each other and began to copulate like animals.

"It will never catch on in Peoria," I said.

I felt the fiery prod in my back again pushing me toward the witch who looked like Ariel. She was standing alone amid the heaps of undulating flesh, looking lost and bewildered.

"You, too," the demon behind me said.

"You're missing out on all the fun," I said, but I winced as the hot points invaded my back.

Under the levity I was ashamed that what was going on around me had aroused me, and that my condition was obvious to everyone who was interested. Orgy may have been the order of the day, but I refused to let myself be submerged in the steaming piles of human and inhuman bodies that lay everywhere around the clearing. It may have been only a dream, but one must maintain standards even in dreams. And even in a dream I felt that my decision was important, that if I allowed myself to be tempted I was doomed.

"Go on," the voice behind me said. "She's available. Everybody's doing it."

The witch looked at me appealingly, but what she was appealing for I didn't know.

"Get at it," the demon said in my ear. "You want to, and wanting to is as bad as doing it. Besides, he who hesitates, you know." And he began describing, in the lewdest terms imaginable, what I could do with the witch.

I cut him off. I swung my arm around and hit him a solid blow to the head. "Never!" I said, and he reeled away, a look of surprise twisting his demonic face.

"Then I shall!" Satan howled, and let the limp body of the lady fall to the ground. He turned to the witch who looked like Ariel. "Come, honey-sweet virgin," he said in a mockery of tenderness. "Come, dear timid girl. Come, innocent. Come to your lover, your bridegroom, your lord . . ."

As the hairy arms wrapped around her white body and the leathery wings enclosed them both in a horrible embrace, I noticed what I had not seen before—the remarkable resemblance of Satan to Solomon Magus. The hairy fur on the body was like evening clothes. The goatlike legs were like trousers. Even the face seemed less demonic and more like the Magus.

Even while I was thinking this, I was charging forward in a quixotic attempt to rescue a dream witch from a nightmare Devil, but before I could take more than a few steps a pain like fire entered my body from behind. I felt myself lifted into the air and carried, as if by pitchfork, toward the giant fire. Bells began to ring around me as I was thrown toward the flames, and I held up my hands in front of my face to save it for one last moment. . . .

Chapter 9

Now o'er the one half-world
Nature seems dead, and wicked dreams abuse
The curtain'd sleep; witchcraft celebrates
Pale Hecate's offerings; and wither'd murder
Alarm'd by his sentinel, the wolf,
Whose howl's his watch, thus with his stealthy pace,
With Tarquin's ravishing strides, toward his design
Moves like a ghost.

Shakespeare, Macbeth

The insistent ringing of the telephone brought me out of my anguished sleep. I still felt the bite of a fiery pitchfork in my back and the scorch of the flames on my face as I fumbled for the instrument, knocked the handset out of the cradle, picked it up, got the mouthpiece to my ear, switched it around, and mumbled, "Hello? Hello?"

An almost soundless whisper came to my ear. "There is danger." Danger! Of course, and I've just been in it. "A message is in your box. It would be wise to act on it."

"Hello? *Hello?*" I said.

The line was silent, but I thought, half asleep as I was, that I could hear someone breathing. But that was probably me, still out of breath from my recent nightmare.

"Who is this?" I asked.

I got no answer.

I dropped the phone back into the cradle and rolled over and went back to sleep, and back to my dreams. This time the dream was different. This time I felt no sense of the supernatural, no feeling of hovering above a scene of medieval terror; instead I found myself walking along dark corridors toward some unseen, unknown, but horrible goal. The traditional nightmare: I didn't know where I was going, but I knew it was something that would scare me out of my wits.

The sensations in this one, too, were very real. I felt carpets under my feet although I could not see them. I smelled a hint of wood smoke and perhaps a subtler odor of hot wax. But I walked in silence except for my own cautious breathing and the soft fall of shoe on carpet.

I wanted to turn and go the other way, out of the darkness, away from the corridors, into the open and the light, but something pushed me on or drew me forward, the way it happens in nightmares. I kept expecting to come upon something dreadful, some slavering monster or some deadly pitfall, snakes rustling in the dark or spiders dropping from ceilings, or something subtler and more terrible, but nothing opened in front of me but unending corridors winding and turning, branching and coming together, until at last I decided I must be in some Minotaurish maze, and my fate was to be doomed to wander here until I starved—or woke up.

At this thought I advanced more boldly, preferring to happen upon a physical threat rather than spend the whole nightmare fearing one. If something were drawing me on, it wasn't doing a very good job of guidance. I willed myself onward toward the ominous end. Sometimes people can do that in dreams. I read once that a primitive Malayan tribe, the Senoi, spends most of its time doing that; the children tell their dreams to their elders, and the elders sit around analyzing them like Freud himself, and they train their children to control their dreams so that they become the supreme rulers and masters of their own dream universes. They learn to control their dreams in a way that is seldom possible to Western man.

I don't know if all this is true, but in my dream, at least, I found the path in front of me beginning to lighten. In a moment lighted candles appeared in wall-mounted sconces. By their flickering illumination I began to notice the carpets; they seemed to be woven of silk, in blue and red and green and yellow, like Oriental or Persian rugs. The walls were hung with pictures and tapestries; some of them seemed to be quite good, though old-fashioned. Antiques, perhaps.

The corridors, however, had no doors in them or any apparent purpose except to lead me toward some point in time and space that I could not avoid, although I did not want to be there. By these signs I knew for certain that this was a dream. There are no real places like this; they exist only inside the head.

I willed again that I might find whatever waited for me at the end of these corridors. Within a few moments the corridor brightened further. I saw a door ahead. The smell of wood smoke was stronger here, but there were other odors, too: chemicals, perfumes . . . I could hear a voice or voices rising and falling rhythmically. As I got closer to the door, I realized that the sound was a voice chanting; it was coming from beyond the door, and it resembled the Catholic Mass in Latin.

The door was well oiled for a dream door. It opened noiselessly, and I eased it away from me, cautious even in my dreams. Beyond was darkness, but the darkness was not complete. A fringe of light lay along the floor like gold lace. Some kind of curtains or tapestry covered the other side. I slipped into the room and gently pulled the door shut behind me. I turned the handle a couple of times to make sure I could get out that way in a hurry if I had to. Carefully, then, I parted hangings and looked into a seventeenth-century French chapel. Well, I didn't know for sure it was seventeenth century, but it was old. I could tell it was French by the legends in the two stained-glass windows on either side of the room. And I knew it was a chapel because it had an altar in it.

The altar was in the center of the room. Several easy chairs stood in front of it; cushions were placed on the floor for the comfort of the well-to-do family whose chapel this was. Asceticism was not one of the virtues their chaplain often preached about, I guessed. If their chaplain was the person presiding at the ceremony now, I could understand why.

He was the ugliest priest I had ever seen. He was an old man who had lived a self-indulgent life. He was tall and fat in his ceremonial regalia. Blue veins stood out on his bloated, sensual face, and one of his eyes squinted malignly. He was the one who had been chanting.

Black candles were lighted in twin candelabra that stood behind him. A mattress had been placed on the altar, and a woman lay crossways on the mattress, facing the priest. It wasn't just any woman. It was a naked woman. She was face up, her legs dangling over the edge of the mattress, and she was Catherine La Voisin, her hair as bright on the pillow as the fire that burned in the fireplace at the far end of the room, and her body was as spectacularly female as it had appeared clothed in the Crystal Room.

Her arms were stretched out in the form of a cross, though her fists were clenched. Just beyond her hands black candles burned. A cross was upside down between her breasts, and a chalice rested uneasily upon her belly.

I was some twenty feet from the altar and I didn't dare separate the hangings enough to get a good view, so I didn't see everything that was going on. But I saw more than I wanted to see. The chalice on La Voisin's belly was dripping with some kind of dark-red fluid. I hoped it was grape juice or wine, but I had no confidence in that, because I thought I saw a tiny human foot extended still and pale beyond the edge of the altar, and the stains around the mouths of La Voisin and the priest were more rust-colored than purple.

The chanting went on, interrupted only by various ceremonial actions. The priest, for instance, kissed La Voisin's naked body a lot, lifted and lowered a small black wafer which both he and La Voisin tasted, and did much other lewdness that I was glad was hidden from me. I should have turned away, but I couldn't move. That's the way it is with dreams.

It was all done with ritual significance and devout belief, and it should have sickened me, even in my dream. It did, in a way. But it affected me in another way as well. La Voisin's female characteristics were a caricature of what men are supposed to find irresistible in a woman, and they didn't attract me. Not really. Well, maybe in a kind of symbolic sense, as a caricature, like a men's magazine cartoon. And yet I found myself aroused, as I had been at the witches' Sabbath, in spite of my best intentions. Except this time it was focused on the naked body and abundant flesh of La Voisin.

I saw her head turn toward the hangings behind which I looked out upon the sacrilegious scene. I saw her eyes widen with surprise and her lips curl with delight. I didn't understand how she could see anything, or recognize anyone she might glimpse, and then I realized that I was no longer behind the hangings, I was in front of them, and I was walking toward the altar, walking toward the perverted priest and the desecrated altar, walking toward the naked body of La Voisin with the single intention of consummating upon the altar the terrible thing that had been going on here in this room.

La Voisin removed the chalice from her belly like any practical woman, and held out her arms to me. I saw a few blond hairs fall from one hand, and I moved toward her arms, forgetful of everything and everyone but the aching need for her. . . .

And I woke with the feeling that the telephone had been ringing just before I wakened. Now it was still. Had I dreamed it? Or had the recent dream all happened in the instant after I had hung up the telephone? If that telephone message had been real and not a dream . . .

I still remembered the lust I had felt for the red witch. My body still remembered, and I wondered about the sanity of my subconscious. Was I perverted enough to really, subconsciously, desire such an encounter? Were my conscious censors suppressing the real me? Was I really a monster? I hadn't resisted the way I did in the previous dream.

Maybe both dreams were the natural result of too much incredible experience and too much reading in strange books before I fell asleep. After all, a person isn't responsible for the lewdness of his dreams, is he? I had the sickening feeling that I was. Because I still lusted for the red witch, inexplicably, against reason, knowing that her touch was, perhaps, truly a fate worse than death.

Maybe, I thought, the dreams were attempts by my subconscious to warn me about my weaknesses, about the danger they might place me in.

Danger! That's what the telephone call had said. Danger, all right. I still felt the places where the nightmare pitchfork had pierced my back and my face still remembered the flames.

I looked at the telephone. Had that happened? I was beginning to doubt everything. I picked up the handset and dialed O.

"This is the operator," a woman's voice said. I didn't recognize it. Why should I recognize it? I was beginning to think that everything was something else in disguise. "What can I do for you?"

What, indeed? An answer? A word of sanity? "Could you tell me if I received a telephone call this morning?" I asked.

"Room number, please?"

"Seven oh seven."

"There have been no incoming messages," she said.

Of course. There would be no record of messages dialed

within the hotel. So the answer meant nothing. "Thanks," I said and eased the phone down.

I looked at my watch. It was not quite eight, but I was wide awake. No use trying to get back to sleep, even if I wanted to. I rubbed my face. I didn't think I wanted to.

I thought of Ariel and smiled. I felt warm inside when I thought about her. It wasn't like my dream about La Voisin, but nicer in a way. She was a sweet kid—well, not exactly a kid, I amended as I remembered how she had looked in this room—and she was caught in a worse mess than I was. I was just on the fringes, but she was in the middle of it, and there was no way out for her. It was unfair. She was just a poor, frightened girl, and, by everything I held sacred, I would get her out of this and then—and then—

I caught myself. *Poor, frightened girl? Don't kid yourself, Casey! She's a witch, a real, honest-to-goodness witch, and she makes things happen that no normal person can do. Casey Kingman to the rescue, my aching back! Watch your romantic notions, boy!*

But what a witch! I mused.

Come off it, Casey! I told myself sternly. *What's the matter with you? Do you think you're in love with this girl, a girl who won't level with you, a girl who won't even give you her right name? Old footloose, love-'em-and-leave-'em Casey?*

I nodded. And that sat me straight up in bed. Could I be in love with Ariel? I had to admit that I could.

Well, I thought, worse things could happen to a man. Like being mated to a witch on an altar or being pitchforked into a fire by a demon.

I looked at the telephone again. A note in my box? I

picked up the handset and dialed the desk. Charlie answered.

"How did you get registered here?" he asked indignantly.

"Never mind that!" I snapped, and I thought of a story I could tell him that would make his few remaining hairs stand on end. Charlie and his precious hotel! "Is there a message for me—room seven oh seven?"

"Just a minute," he snapped back.

I waited.

"As a matter of fact, there is. Want me to read it to you?"

"Isn't it sealed?"

"Just a slip of paper. Not even folded."

"Don't you put messages in envelopes?" I asked.

"Yes," he said impatiently, "we put messages in envelopes, but whoever put this message in your box didn't put it in an envelope. Do you want me to read it or not?"

"All right. What does it say?"

"On one side it says 'seven oh seven.' "

"Okay, okay. That's me."

"On the other it says 'eleven eleven.' What is this, Casey? Are you playing games again?"

"Not me," I protested. "How do you know the message isn't 'seven oh seven' for 'eleven eleven'?"

"How should I know? I didn't put it there."

"Who did?"

"The night clerk, I guess."

"You're a big help," I told him, and hung up.

So there was a message, and maybe someone in the hotel had left it for me and had called me to tell me about it. But how had they known my room number? They could have called the desk. But how had they known my name? Or maybe this magic business had a recoil to it. Maybe my subconscious reached out to gather that information, cryptic as it was, and then put in a call to my conscious mind.

"Hello, Conscious. Are you there?"

"Just barely. Right now I'm about to be tossed from a pitchfork into a fire. Who is this?"

"This is your Subconscious."

"Well, well, Subconscious. Imagine hearing from you. How the hell are things down there?"

"Cluttered, boy. Pretty messy. You've really got to do something about all these nasty things lying around all over. I trip over something new every time I try to move around. Somebody's got to get busy in here with a shovel or a fire hose or something—"

"Did you call me at a time like this just to complain about—?"

"Sorry, Conscious, but if you had to live in conditions like this maybe you'd— All right, all right. You've got to wake up. You're in danger, and I just learned there's a message for you downstairs. So get off that nightmare and get on your horse, boy!"

And then, of course, the conscious mind rolls back over and goes back to sleep. How does that sound? I thought it sounded lousy. Maybe it was coincidence. Or maybe somebody had called me. With the wild talents running loose around this hotel, it should be a simple matter to put in a call to a person going under the name of Gabriel. Or, for that matter, I thought with sudden comfort, it could have been Ariel calling; she knew my room number.

I turned it over and over as I let a cold shower bring me fully awake, shaved hurriedly with a razor I had picked up last night in the hotel drugstore, and reluctantly put on the clothes I had worn yesterday.

Eleven eleven. Obviously a room number. Too obviously. Or was I being too subtle? A date? What happened in eleven eleven? Nothing. The Normans conquered England in ten sixty-six, and King John signed the Magna Carta in twelve fifteen, but nothing happened in eleven eleven. November eleventh? That was more than a week ahead, and what did it matter? This problem would be over by then, or we all would be dead, wasted away, perhaps, like Ariel's father. A room number, then. Whose? Ariel's? That was logical. But why should there be danger there? It could be a trap. Maybe it was Solomon's room, or La Voisin's, or maybe I would find myself in a trap like the black mirror from which I could not extract myself.

I shrugged. There was danger in excess caution, too, and a man could speculate himself into a hole. I strapped on my shoulder holster and inspected the clip. I felt a little safer as I slipped the gun back. Maybe I was foolish, but I had a hunch Betsy might come in handy before the day was over. She wasn't subtle and she didn't know the first thing about magic, but when she spoke, people listened.

I hid Uriel's manuscript, hesitated at the door, and returned for a piece of chalk. I jotted an equation across the inside of the door, making certain that it crossed onto the door frame. I stepped out into the hall, closed the door behind me, and heard it latch. If magic still worked, that should keep everybody out, including hotel employees.

I waited a few minutes for an elevator. When the doors opened in front of me, I walked right in, proud of myself—not for refusing to consider the possibility that the elevator was only an illusion but for walking into it even though I thought it might be only an elevator shaft waiting for me. I pushed the button marked 11. When the elevator stopped and the doors opened, I stepped out into a corridor just like my own.

The door across the corridor was marked 1100, and arrows pointed left and right with appropriate numbers in the eleven hundreds printed in the fat middle of the arrows. But all that could have been a trick. I didn't believe anything any more.

Eleven eleven was down the corridor to the right and just around a corner. I took a deep breath, grabbed the doorknob, and turned it. Something snapped. The door swung open.

I looked at the sun-bright room for a long moment before I understood what was going on.

"My God!" I said, my voice quivering with horror. "Ariel!"

Chapter 10

The mind is its own place, and in it self
Can make a Heav'n of Hell, a Hell of Heav'n.

John Milton, Paradise Lost

She was still in her nightgown, and the face she turned up to me was twisted with guilt, and some other emotion I could not read. In her hands, as she sat cross-legged upon the floor, was a little waxen figure. Even if I had not seen the blond hairs pressed into the tiny head, I would have known who the figure was supposed to represent. Me.

Her hands were still busy, winding darker hairs around the chest of the mommet. In the window, directly in the sunlight, were two other figures. One was made of a darker material. Around its chest was a red hair. Next to it was a wax image that the sun had half-melted into a puddle.

Strangest of all was Ariel. Before I had thought her only pretty. Now I knew that she was the most beautiful woman I had ever seen, and my throat ached with loving her, and my arms twitched with the desire to gather her up in them.

"Oh, no!" I said, and turned away, my hands thrown up to cover my face, as if by this gesture I could shut out the scene I had stumbled upon.

"Wait, Gabriel!" she said urgently, her silence suddenly broken. "Wait! You don't understand!"

I moved away blindly. What could she say to change what I had seen? She muttered something behind me. I stopped, not because I wanted to but because suddenly I couldn't move. I was fixed to the spot like Lot's wife or like all those foolish men who looked at Medusa's snaky locks. Then I could move my hands, and I took them away from my face, and I was inside the room and the door was closed.

Ariel was standing. Her look of guilt had changed to annoyance, as if I were the one who had done something wrong. "Oh, why did you have to break in here now?"

"Ariel!" I exclaimed. "Why? Why are you doing this? I thought we were working together, and now I find you making wax images of me. It's fantastic. It's terrible! Why are you doing this to me? My God, Ariel, you'd think after what we've been through together, after last night—"

"For goodness' sake, shut up!" she said, her annoyance replaced by bewilderment. "What in the name of— What do you think I'm doing?"

"Look!" I said, trying to point to the images slowly melting in the window, and failing. "You've been trying to kill me! But why?"

Slowly, irresistibly, a smile spread over her beautiful face. She started to laugh. It bubbled out of her uncontrollably. She fell across the bed and howled. I watched her with growing irritation as my anger and horror faded. I didn't see anything funny about it."

"Kill you, Gabriel?" she gasped. "Only with love. Oh, no, Gabriel. Not you. Anybody but you."

"Well, then," I snapped in my best schoolteacherish manner that had straightened up the most giggly of girls, "what's the meaning of all this?"

She sat up in the bed, suddenly sobered, studying my face as if she wasn't sure how I would react. "It's a love spell," she said, and then she couldn't look at me any more.

"A love spell!" I repeated. And I recognized instantly that it was true. I loved her madly, infinitely, eternally. She was the most precious thing in the world. It would be ecstasy to die for her, and I would spend the rest of my life keeping anything from harming her, from troubling her for an instant. "But all these images—"

"They were part of it. The wax one there, the one melting in the sun, that made your heart soften toward me."

"It wasn't exactly hardened before," I pointed out.

"I know that," she said, "but I didn't want to take any chances. The clay image that is hardening is intended to harden your heart against La Voisin." She laughed. "You should have seen me earlier, when I was chanting."

"But why did you do all this?" I asked. "You didn't have to use magic to get me to help you."

"Don't you see?" she said quickly, as if she were trying to convince herself as well as me. "I was trying to protect you from La Voisin. When they found out that their mirror trick didn't work, she would have tried a love spell, or an Amatory Mass, rather, since that is the way their minds work."

I shuddered. In love with Catherine La Voisin. I would rather be in love with a black widow spider. I wasn't sure, either, that my feeling was all due to the clay image. And then I thought of something. "I'm not sure that she didn't," I said slowly.

"What do you mean?"

I told her about the dream and the corridors and the strange Mass.

Ariel nodded. "That's what it was. The room you described is like the chapel in which Madame de Montespan had several love Masses performed in order to win and keep Louis XIV. The chapel belonged to a widow named Catherine Deshayes, who was known as La Voisin. And the priest you described sounds very much like the sinister Abbé Guibourg, who performed several of the Masses, just as you described."

"Then it wasn't a dream!" I exclaimed. "How could I have dreamed it like that?" I stopped and thought a moment, my natural skepticism surfacing again. "Unless I read about it last night."

"It could have been real," she said, "and perhaps my clay mommet saved you—"

"From a fate worse than death," we said in unison. "Yeah," I said, "but if that could have been real, and I was really in danger, what about the other dream?" And I told her about the witches' Sabbath.

"I think that really was happening," she said, "in a symbolic sense, anyhow. And that's what magic is, the substitution of a single aspect for the whole, or a resemblance for the real thing. A symbol. Which means you can get killed just as easily by a symbol, or a dream, as by reality."

"But the brooms!" I said. "They were riding the brooms the wrong way, with the straw in front of them—"

"And a candle in the straw?" she completed.

"How did you know?" I demanded.

"That's the way paintings and drawings began to show them beginning early in the seventeenth century."

"I know I didn't read anything about that!" I said.

"Are you sure?" she asked a bit tartly.

"I'm sorry," I said. "All this comes hard." I looked up. "Then you really could have been there, the young witch—"

"Never!" she said, and then her voice softened. "But I'm glad you acted as you did." She sighed and then muttered something. Suddenly the rest of my body was free to move. "You can go now," she said quietly.

I turned toward the door, frowning and feeling unhappy. I didn't like the way I was being pushed around, brought here, involved there, trapped, my feelings changed, and—

Not so fast, boy! What are you complaining about? Why don't you admit it! Ever since you met this girl you've been falling in love with her, long before any spells were said over wax images. Remember last night?

I remembered and smiled.

Maybe the spell had nothing at all to do with the way you feel. Even if it did, it only intensified something that you already felt. So things got hurried up a little. So things got intensified, made more perfect. Have you got a kick coming?

Sure, I've got a kick, I thought, and frowned. *Suppose she isn't in love with me. How about that?*

Come on, Casey! You may be in love, but you don't have to be stupid. You didn't believe everything she said, did you? There must have been simpler ways to protect you against La Voisin. If she went around making men fall in love with her right and left, it would be damned inconvenient for her. See the way she looks at you, boy! Look—

I turned back into the room. Ariel was still sitting on the bed, watching me with big, serious eyes. Of course. It was true. Girls cast love spells over men because they're in love with them. I took three steps toward her and bent down and gathered her in my arms and kissed her passionately.

She stiffened and struggled in strange helplessness for a girl of her powers. Her hands beat a gentle tattoo against my chest. "Stop!" she gasped, when she had freed her lips from mine. "Stop it!"

"I can't," I said. "I can't help myself. Besides, you could always cast another spell if you wanted to."

I gave her a chance, but she didn't say anything. So I kissed her again. Slowly she relaxed. Her arms went around my neck. We sank down onto the bed. I gathered her close to me, knowing I would never be closer to paradise.

Finally she put her head back and sighed. She opened her eyes, her beautiful blue eyes, and whispered, "Then you don't mind?"

"Mind?" I said. "One might as well mind the coming of the seasons, the way the moon turns round the earth, the fact that rain falls down instead of up, the rising of the sun in the east, the singing of the birds, the—"

"Hush!" she said and kissed me.

We sank into another period of rapture, and I discovered that she was proficient in an older and more powerful witchcraft, that she was indeed in love with me, and with a passion as powerful as my own. But she had willpower and I didn't, and finally she fought herself free of my embrace and her desires and sat up, straightening her hair and rearranging her nightgown. I reached for her again, but she pushed my hands away.

"I can see that I'm going to have trouble with you," she said with mock severity. "The Grimoires and the Keys and the Faustbooks are so impractical. They never mention this kind of difficulty."

"You have no one to blame but yourself," I pointed out. "You have bewitched me. I am a slave of passion." I tried to pull her back to my side.

She brushed my hands away and stood up, although I could tell that she did it with difficulty. "I suppose," she said moodily, "but I must remain a virgin."

I sat up at that, frustrated and impatient and as nearly sharp with Ariel as I could ever be. "That doesn't seem quite fair!" I said.

"I don't mean forever," she said.

"You mean you're holding out for marriage," I said unhappily.

"I'm not 'holding out' as you so delicately put it," she snapped, and then her tone softened. "It's not just the morality, and I'm certainly not thinking of marriage right now, but the condition, the physical condition, is of great importance in the practice of magic, and we need all the help we can get. I don't dare lose my virginity while we are in such peril."

"And was there any danger of that?" I asked.

She caught her breath. "Oh, you know," she said softly. "You *know*."

I controlled myself and stood up. I crossed my arms and moved a few feet away. "Did you work that spell just to save me from La Voisin?"

Her eyes widened innocently. "Why, what other reason could I have?"

I growled and lunged at her, but she jumped out of my way and evaded me easily. "You beautiful witch!" I said, panting as I tried to corner her. "You must have known what would happen when you put your room number in my box."

She stopped running. I caught her, almost knocking her to the floor. We stood, swaying like poplars caught in a storm, her face upturned to mine, wide-eyed and afraid.

"I didn't put anything in your box," she said.

We were still pressed close, but the half-controlled urgency of passion no longer bound us. Around us the almost forgotten forces of evil were closing in, and for a moment our closeness was our only protection.

"They must have done it," I said. "At least we can thank them for this—they brought us together and let us discover how we feel about each other."

"Maybe," she said. She was trembling a little in my arms. That bothered me. She had always been the steady one. "If they did it to drive us apart. If they wanted you to find me working spells."

"Why else?"

She shook her head. "I don't know. They're devious and nasty, as you discovered. Suddenly I'm afraid."

I bent down and kissed her lips. Not like before. Gently. Her lips were cold. "The frightened witch!" I said, to chide her back into courage. "Don't be afraid! This was their second mistake. We'll prove it to them. They can't beat us now."

She raised her head and smiled. She was a magnificent woman, even if she was a witch, and I had more reasons to be proud of her every time we met.

"Listen," I said. "We need a council of war. Can you get hold of Uriel?" She nodded. "Bring him down to my room, then. Seven oh seven. Half an hour. Okay?"

She nodded again. I released her, stepped back, and looked at her with fond and possessive eyes. "I love you, Ariel," I said. "I don't think the dolls had anything to do with it, but I don't care if they did."

"I love you," she whispered, "and there wasn't any witchcraft about that. Was there?" she asked suddenly. I held out my hands helplessly, and she laughed. She got serious again. "I'll remove the spell." I shrugged to show that I didn't believe in spells even now. "No," she went on, "I want to. Not because of you. For me. I want to be sure it's real. I want you to love me for myself."

"Don't you dare!" I said, as my disbelief crumbled with a shudder. "Do you think I want to take a chance on losing this—this way I feel? But," I added wryly, "I'd appreciate your keeping those dolls in a safe place. I wouldn't want them falling into just anybody's hands."

I closed the door gently behind me, feeling as if I were leaving a treasure that only I knew about, that only I appreciated. I felt too good to wait for the elevator. For the moment I forgot my distrust of stairs, and I ran down four flights, three steps at a time. I ran out into the hall and slowed to a walk as a well-dressed elderly couple passed on their way to the elevator. I could feel them turning to stare at me.

"It's magic," I hummed.

The woman sniffed.

I reached the door, inserted the key, and turned it. The door didn't open. I turned the handle and pushed. It was stuck as tightly as if it had been boarded up from inside. I glanced at the room number to make certain I had the right room, and then I remembered my precautions. I took the piece of chalk out of my coat pocket and scribbled another equation on the front of the door. Added together, the two equations canceled each other. Their sum was zero.

The door swung open. I scrubbed the figures off both sides of the door with the heel of my hand, stepped into the room, and closed the door behind me. I fastened the chain latch and spun around, checking the room carefully for any changes. Everything was just as I had left it, down to the smudged circle on the rug.

I stood there, just inside the door, reliving the experiences of the morning, the pain and the joy, and feeling great, feeling that we would win, that events were breaking our way. I had no doubts about that. All that was left was a little detail work.

Ariel! My body got warm as I remembered the beauty of her face, the sweetness of her lips, and the fire of her body, a perfect combination of youthful firmness and womanly softness. And the wonder of it all, the abiding wonder, was Ariel herself, an understanding, gentle, delightful—

To the showers, Casey!

"Showers?"

A cold, cold shower is what you need. Icy, in fact.

"I've had a shower this morning!"

That isn't the kind I meant, and you know it.

"Really, now. What's the harm—?"

Just because you're in love with a nice girl and you think she's in love with you—

"What do you mean, 'think'?"

All right—and a nice girl's in love with you, don't forget that you're not one step closer to discovering Solomon's identity. And until you've discovered that, you're not walking on clouds. You're walking on quicksand.

The water was pure ice. It hit my body like sleet. I endured it as long as I could, puffing and blowing and gasping, and feeling virtuous, gaining points for every second I stood under the shower head. Finally I reached blindly for the towel. As I reached I remembered the feeling of uneasiness that had come over me as I entered the bathroom. Suddenly I knew why. When I had left, the towels had been used and disarranged. When I came back, everything had been straightened up. Someone had been in the room since I had left; someone had been in the bathroom. Not the maid; she couldn't get in. Someone dumb, dumb enough to arrange the towels neatly. But I was dumber.

All the awareness was too late. The towel that I had raised to dry my face had slipped through my fingers like silk. It coiled itself around my neck. It tightened with the strength of a full-grown boa constrictor. I stumbled out of the shower, tugging at it with both hands, my face purpling, my lungs struggling for breath.

I staggered and slipped across the tile floor. The room was beginning to turn red. The need for air was a frantic burning in my chest. I knew it was useless to struggle with this bewitched thing around my neck, but I couldn't give up. I had too much to live for.

Fool! Fool! Half an hour, you told her, and it hasn't been fifteen minutes. And if she should arrive early, the door is locked and chained. Better to be stupid than half smart!

The redness darkened. I staggered and almost fell. Life curdled in my chest.

You can't fight magic with ordinary strength, Casey! Think, man, think! There must be a counter-spell if you can just think clearly. Think!

But I couldn't think. The darkness invaded my mind like conquering slugs, and as they closed in I thought of Ariel, I thought of her sorrow and despair when she saw my body, and I grieved for her.

And then the last light went out.

Chapter 11

Our trouble in the past has been poor communication between intelligence and instinct, which has meant that the intelligent people lacked power and vitality, while the instinctive people lacked vision and long-distance purpose.

Colin Wilson, The Occult

I dreamed that I was drowning in a lake. Every time I came to the surface to get a breath of air, a hand would push me back down into the water. Or a foot, a woman's foot with a shoe on it. I knew it was a woman's foot because it had a high heel, and I got a glimpse of a shapely leg above it.

Finally I stayed above the water long enough to shake the moisture from my eyes and recognize the woman who was sitting on a yellow rubber raft in the middle of the lake. It was Suzie. She was wearing a black string bikini, and she did great things for it, though what she was doing on a rubber raft in a string bikini wearing high heels I couldn't figure out. Nor why she kept pushing me back under the water, though I finally decided it all had some Freudian significance.

Kick. Bubble. Splash. Gasp.

Finally I got the lake out of my throat long enough to ask Suzie what she was doing here.

"I've got some new friends," she said.

Kick. Bubble. Splash. Gasp.

"What kind of friends?" I asked fluidly.

"They're a strange bunch," she said, "but they're very rich, and they have all kinds of unusual abilities."

Kick. Bubble. Splash. Gasp.

"What kind of abilities, Suzie?" I asked.

"You know. They can give you good luck or bad luck, whichever they wish. They live in these turn-of-the-century apartments, uptown. You'd never suspect."

Kick. Bubble. Splash. Gasp.

"What do they want with you, Suzie?"

"They keep bringing around this horny gentleman when they think I'm too stoned to know."

Kick. Bubble. Splash. Gasp.

"Why do you put up with it, Suzie?"

"They treat me like I was the queen mother-to-be, or something. And this rough, scaly character is the king. You know?" She always used to say "you know" too much. But she had a great body.

Kick. Bubble. Splash. Gasp.

"They're Satanists, Suzie. They're using you as a breeder, to give birth to a new reign of evil on earth. 'What rough beast,' you know." I got into the habit of saying it, too, when I was around her.

"I know that," she said sulkily. "Do you think I'm stupid or something? They keep feeding me some kind of ground-up root. But I've got them fooled."

Kick. Bubble. Splash. Gasp.

"How's that, Suzie?" What I could see of her looked great, I had to admit. The life apparently was agreeing with her.

"I've got a secret supply of birth-control pills. Think I

want a brat? All little kids are devils, of course, but this is ridiculous!"

Kick. Bubble. Splash. Gasp.

"Suzie," I said, as I came up, "I've been wanting to ask you something."

"So ask," she said.

Kick. Bubble. Splash. Gasp.

"Why are you doing this to me?"

"It's all Freudian," she said. "You know? This lake is the womb, and you're struggling to be born, and I don't want another brat—"

"Oh, the hell with it!" I said, and sank of my own volition. Fluid filled my eyes and lungs and all the empty places of my body, my stomach and bowels and sinuses and even the hollow bones. . . .

"Well, young man," someone said, "are you going to wake up or do I have to drown you?"

I opened my eyes, spluttering, and breathed deeply. The air went into my lungs like live steam, but I was so surprised and so grateful to be breathing again that I didn't care. I raised my hands and massaged my throat, wincing. It was wet, like my face.

"Ah," said the voice, "that's better." It was a woman's voice, and I knew that I should recognize it.

I turned my head in that direction. "You!" I said. It wasn't very gracious, but it was all I could think of, and it came out in a croak. She was standing beside the bed, an empty water glass in her hand.

It was Mrs. Peabody. I hadn't even thought of Mrs. Peabody that day, and here she was, her gray curls bobbing as she nodded vigorously. "And a lucky thing for you that it was. Another minute and you'd have been beyond caring."

I turned my head back and forth, wondering if it was going to fall off. Apparently it wasn't. My circumstances began to interest me a bit more after I decided that I was going to live.

I was lying on the bed. I was cold. I was naked and wet, which was why I was cold. The towel that had tried to strangle me and had very nearly succeeded was lying across me, lifeless but strategic.

Mrs. Peabody chuckled. She seemed to be enjoying the whole thing, and I resented it. "Is this the way you greet all your female guests? Well, don't lie there lewd and naked all day. Put on some clothes!"

I sat up, clutching the towel. "You might at least turn your back," I said.

"You can't show me anything I haven't seen before," she said. "Even here in this room. After all, that towel was around your neck when I came in."

"Okay," I said, and dropped the towel to slip into my clothes. She quickly turned her back and pretended to stare out the window at a dingy ventilation shaft filled with pigeon droppings. "How did you get in?" I asked hoarsely. "I'm not complaining, you understand," I added quickly.

"Same way your other visitors got in," she said. "You may have had your door locked, but you left another doorway wide open." She pointed at the center of the rug.

There was the circle I had drawn last night, the circle in which Ariel had appeared and disappeared twice, one arc of it scuffed out by someone's foot.

"You're a very careless young man," the little old lady

said, turning around abruptly to confront me. I turned my back to her and hastily zipped up my pants. There was no logic to it, but the act of zipping seemed better done in private. "Carelessness is always dangerous," she went on, "but when you get to fooling around with magic and witchcraft, it becomes downright foolhardy."

"You didn't ask me about my capacity for carelessness when you talked to me about the job," I said with a note of reproach, "any more than you warned me that I would be fooling around with magic and witchcraft."

"Speaking of the job," she said, getting away untouched, "what have you found out?"

The question caught me flatfooted. I blinked twice. "Nothing," I said.

"Wasted my money, did I?" She nodded as if she had expected it all along.

"Now, hold on," I objected. "I've been on the case only a little more than twenty-four hours."

"Long enough," she said. The way things had happened she was right, I guess, but I didn't like the way she stamped around the room.

Some of my annoyance must have shown in my voice. "I've got a few complaints myself. You threw me into this situation without a word of explanation. You let me think it was a simple case of shadowing—"

"Would you have believed me if I'd told you the truth?" she asked shrewdly.

"Well, no," I admitted. "But you let me blunder my way around this hotel, nearly getting killed two or three times, or maybe worse, and—"

"Told you there'd be danger."

"Not this kind of danger." I motioned toward the deadly towel.

"You didn't think of that when you were looking at that bill." She chuckled. "All you had in your eyes were zeros. Want to give it back?"

I hesitated and then made up my mind. "All right. Deducting a day's work and expenses." I pulled my billfold out of my right rear pocket.

She held up a pale, thin hand to stop me. "Now, wait just a minute. I haven't said I wanted it back. I just asked if you wanted to give it back. You can't quit a job that easy. What have you found out?"

"I told you," I said. "Nothing." I took the remains of a thousand dollars out of my billfold. Luckily I hadn't used too much of it.

"Didn't find out his name?" she asked spryly.

"Solomon," I said. I started counting the bills again. "Solomon Magus."

"Nonsense," she said impatiently. "You know what I want: his real name."

"No," I said firmly. I counted out nine hundred and seventy-six dollars on the bureau top, picked up the seventy-six dollars to make it an even hundred dollars for the day, and I shoved the rest toward her.

"No clues?" she asked. "No guesses? Is that all I get for my hundred dollars?"

"Well," I said reluctantly, "I found an open airline ticket to Washington, D.C."

"Ah," she said with great significance.

"But I'm not even sure it belongs to him. There's your money. Take it."

Her faded blue eyes looked me over shrewdly. I shifted uncomfortably under their gaze. "You're too eager. Why? Got another client, have you?"

"Maybe," I admitted.

"Who is it?"

"That," I said pointedly, "is none of your business."

"Well," she said, "I reckon until I take that money back you're still working for me, and I reckon I haven't got much so far for my money, and I reckon that it is my business."

"Go to hell!" I said.

"Paying you as well as I am?" she asked curiously. "Bet not. Bet it's a girl," she said, her eyes sparkling. "Paying you in kisses, I bet. You look like the kind of young fool who'd rather have kisses than money."

I thought of Ariel and felt my face get warm. "Maybe you're right," I said. "Good-bye and everything."

"Don't rush me, young man!" she snapped. "I'll go when I'm ready. I'm not sure I want to call you off this case. A bargain's a bargain."

"Only when it's made in good faith—on both sides," I said. "You misled me."

"You're an ungrateful young man," she said, shaking her head in wonderment. "Here I save your life, and now you're tossing me out of your room without even a thank-you. I tell you, it's enough to shake your faith in this younger—"

"I'm sorry," I said, and I was. "I do thank you, but I can't work for you. My new client may show up soon, and I think it would be awkward if you met."

"That's better," she said. "Now. Tell me. Does this new job conflict with what I paid you to do? Eh? Is this new client asking you to do something you couldn't share with me? Eh?"

"Well—" I said, hesitating.

"Then," she said triumphantly, "why not do both jobs at once? You have no real dislike for my money, do you?"

"It's not that—" I began.

"What is it, then?"

I thought about it for a moment and shook my head. "I'm sorry again. I can't take anybody as a client if I don't know their real name."

"Know the girl's real name, eh?" She chuckled again as my face got red. "All right, young man, I won't torment you. If that's the way you want it."

"You won't tell me your real name?" I asked.

She shook her head decisively, picked up the money from the bureau, and walked toward the door. As she unhooked the chain, she turned back. "You can tell that girl for me," she said, "that she's a very lucky woman."

I smiled and looked aside a bit embarrassed, and was turned to stone. Somehow the black mirror that had been leaning against the wall had been turned around so that it faced into the room. The little old lady should have been reflected in it, but it wasn't the little old lady I saw.

Darkly, glimmering up at me through the mists of night, was the face of Ariel.

Chapter 12

Here we may reign secure, and in my choice
To reign is worth ambition though in hell:
Better to reign in hell, than serve in heav'n.

John Milton, Paradise Lost

She turned her head, and I looked into the mirrored eyes of a frightened angel. Dark angel. She could see me, and she knew that I could see her. I looked back and forth between the night-shadowed image of youth and beauty and the reality of withered age. Angel? No, witch. And I loved the one in the black mirror.

"Ariel?" I groaned. "Why? Why? And how do I know which one is you?"

She took a step toward me, the gray-haired little old lady, her hand half raised, and as she did the door swung open behind her. Uriel walked into the room calmly and stopped, glancing once at us and then at the wall where the mirror rested. He may have been old, but he was quick. He grasped the situation almost instantly.

Uriel was only an inch or two taller than the old lady, and his white hair went with her gray, perky curls. They made a jolly old couple. But where did that leave me? In love with a phantom in a dark glass? "For now we see," I recalled, "through a glass, darkly; but then face to face: now I know in part; but then shall I know even as also I am known."

But before that, I thought sadly, is the phrase about putting away childish things. Like love and trust.

A sob broke from the old lady's throat. It was incongruous. Old ladies don't sob. "Don't you know?" she asked, and the voice was Ariel's.

"How *can* I?" I groaned. It was getting to be a habit. "Everybody's someone else. Nobody's themselves. How do I know what to believe? Who are you?"

She broke into tears and sank down in a chair, sobbing. "You don't love me," she said brokenly. "If you loved me you would trust me."

"Look in the mirror, son!" Uriel said firmly. "Not directly. That would be dangerous. Look at me!"

I looked. Uriel was mirrored there. Uriel himself, not someone else. "What is that supposed to tell me?" I asked. "That you're not disguised?"

"Exactly," Uriel said. He walked quickly to the mirror, keeping to one side of it so that he did not see his own reflection, and turned it to the wall. "And that means that the mirror shows people as they are, not as they aren't." He inspected the letters around the blackened back of the mirror. "Interesting," he mused and became engrossed.

I turned to Ariel—and it was Ariel. Mrs. Peabody was gone, but she had left her clothing behind. It looked strange on Ariel. I looked at her face. Her eyes were wet with tears as she looked up at me.

"How old are you?" I asked sternly, unable to keep my doubts from spilling over.

"Twenty-two," she said, her voice breaking.

"Really?"

"Well," she said, "twenty-three."

I sighed. That had the real ring of truth. I would have recognized it in my classroom. And, after my experiences of the past twenty-four hours, I had begun to doubt my ability to recognize truth when I heard it. "But why?" I asked. "Why did you do it?"

"Think, Gabriel!" she said, and her tone of guilt was yielding to a note of impatience. "I didn't want anyone to know that I was investigating Solomon. And I certainly had no way of knowing that I could trust you."

"Not at first," I said doggedly. I may not be the quickest guy but I'm persistent. "But you had plenty of chances to tell me later."

She blushed. "I was going to tell you, Gabriel. I was all ready to tell you when I came down here. And then when I knocked and couldn't get an answer, and I had to materialize inside your room and saw you with your face all purple—I decided it would be better for Mrs. Peabody to save you. You would never have to know that I had—concealed my identity the first time we met, and Mrs. Peabody could just fade away."

"And then you had to make one last test to be sure you could trust me," I added, scowling.

"If I'd known you were going to act like this, Gabriel, I'd never have bothered," she retorted, her chin up stubbornly, with supreme illogic.

It was unfair, and I couldn't stand it any longer. "And for God's sake!" I shouted. "Stop calling me Gabriel! You know my name—"

Her eyes widened with alarm. "Be quiet!" she said. "Don't say it!"

I went toward her with some high-class illogic of my own, my arms outstretched to bring her close to me. "Then you do care," I sighed.

The next thing I knew, I was sitting in the chair and she was curled up in my lap, her head on my shoulder, whispering in my ear all the things she had liked about me from the beginning and all the other qualities she had grown to appreciate, and Uriel was coughing, having spent as much time inspecting the mirror as he could justify.

"Children," he said. "Children, we have work to do. And, Ariel, I must tell you, in all kindness, that you are growing quite careless about your spells."

"My goodness," Ariel said, sitting up and looking down at her dress—Mrs. Peabody's dress, that is. "This lavender and lace doesn't do a thing for me, either. You'll have to excuse me for a moment." She leaped from my lap, jumped into the circle, and disappeared.

Uriel and I stared blankly at each other. I shook my head. "Why didn't she just work a spell, the way she did when she changed into Mrs. Peabody?" I asked. Uriel looked puzzled. But I already knew the answer. Whoever heard of a woman deciding what to wear right on the spot?

Ten minutes later she was back inside the circle in tan slacks and a knit top that did a great deal for her, but Uriel and I, under a gentleman's agreement, ignored her appearance and continued our discussion of the books he had noticed on the desk. He had already cleared up a number of my vaguer conceptions about the principles of magic.

Ariel sat down on the edge of a chair, looking hopefully back and forth between us, like a little girl trying not to be heard but seen. At last she gave up. "I'm back," she said.

I turned to her. "Who was Gabriel?"

She sighed heavily. I forced back a smile. "He was Father's protégé, a graduate student who had become virtually an adept. Uriel thought that Gabriel was almost as good as he was himself."

"That's right," Uriel said. "I can't understand—"

"We were hoping that Gabriel could help us against Solomon," Ariel continued. "And then he was killed in a traffic accident."

"That was no accident," I said, and I told them about La Voisin's mistake.

"It was murder, then!" Ariel said angrily. "They're not only power-mad and vicious, they're capable of murder for profit."

"Was Gabriel in love with you?" I asked.

"Maybe," Ariel admitted. "But I didn't— I mean he was just a nice boy. There was nothing—"

"That makes two murders, then," I said. "Gabriel and your father."

"If Prospero's death was murder," Uriel said, shaking his head in disbelief. "I didn't realize anything was wrong until too late. He didn't tell me. He wouldn't talk about his health. But I can't believe that even Solomon would stoop to all the foul, disgusting nonsense involved in the Black Mass, the ruined church, the black Host, the water from the well in which an unbaptized infant has been drowned, and all the rest."

"He has already made two attempts on Gabri—on *his* life," Ariel said. "That black mirror was one and there was an enchanted towel that almost strangled him. And there were two dreams—"

"Dreams?" Uriel repeated, sitting up straight.

"A witches' Sabbath and an Amatory Mass," Ariel said, and told Uriel about the dreams.

Uriel's agitation increased, and I began to feel more nervous about the experiences than I had felt when they were happening. "You mean they were real?" I asked.

Uriel's pale hands fluttered in the air. "Real. Unreal. The terms cease to have meanings. In the world of magic everything has significance; everything stands for something else. Looks can injure and words can kill and dreams can be more dangerous than anything."

"We have to be realistic about what we're facing," Ariel said, getting up to pace in front of us. In spite of myself I couldn't keep a look of admiration out of my eyes at the way she fitted into those slacks and knit top. "The only thing Solomon cares about is power, and the only way he can be sure of that is to kill all of us."

"Oh, dear," Uriel said.

"And I understand that you haven't been feeling well," I said to Uriel while I massaged my throat reminiscently.

"Nonsense," Uriel said stoutly. "Never felt better in my life." But he started coughing, and his cough had a hollow sound. I looked at him closely for perhaps the first time. Now I noticed that Uriel's rosy appearance of health was an illusion. His red cheeks were rouged. I looked at Ariel and found her looking at Uriel with the same concern.

"Ariel said we had to be realistic," I said quietly, "and if we're going to be realistic we're going to have to admit that our chances of succeeding against all of them are almost nonexistent. What if we should give up this impossible battle, check out of the hotel, go underground—" I stopped.

Ariel and Uriel were looking at me with eyes that utterly lacked comprehension.

"You don't mean that!" Ariel said.

"You can't be serious!" Uriel said simultaneously.

I lifted my shoulders and spread out my hands in a gesture of helplessness. "Realistically—" I began.

"Realistically," Ariel echoed. "I meant that we needed to cast aside any illusions about our opponent, not that we should use our difficult situation as an excuse for cowardice."

"What you suggest," Uriel said, "is impossible. It would leave the society to Solomon, to twist it any way he wished. They would all yield to his desires, and we would find ourselves living in a darker world than we had ever imagined."

"He would never be satisfied to leave us alone," Ariel added. "Before he did anything else he would use all the resources of the society to hunt us out, to do away with us."

"Prospero and I thought of the Art as a way of making the world better," Uriel said. "Of providing the energy and the capabilities of another world and another way of thinking to solving the problems that threaten to send humanity back into ignorance and savagery. But if Solomon gets full control of the powers he seeks, we will see ignorance and savagery triumphant. The evil that emerges as an aberration in a rational world will be unleashed. Demons and devils will roam at will across the world commanded by those who are strong enough and served by those who are weak. The darkest ages of human history will seem like arcadias compared to the world that Solomon would create. Satan would be triumphant."

I stared at Uriel's eloquence. "I thought you didn't believe in demons and such superstitions."

Uriel's manner immediately returned to the practical. "The term," he said, "is a convenient fiction for the unseen, and until now unknowable, forces which permeate the universe and can be tapped and controlled by man's mind and will; just as 'electrons' are a convenient fiction to describe the mysterious but controllable energies of electricity."

"We must stop Solomon now," Ariel said, "while we still have a chance."

I lifted my hands defensively. "Okay, okay. I'm convinced. What do we do first?"

Ariel nodded briskly. "Let's get to work. Tell him about the clue, Gabri—"

She stopped and stared at the expression on my face. Something had just occurred to me, and it showed. "You might as well call me Casey," I said. "I just remembered. I signed the hotel register that way."

They stared at me horrified.

I shook my head remorsefully. "I'm afraid I'm a bust at this business. I'll never remember all the rules. I suppose they know your name," I said to Uriel.

"I'm afraid they do," he said. "Since Professor Reeves and I founded the society, we had little opportunity for concealment. Many early members knew us personally, and our preliminary research reports attracted a little publicity. Anyone could have learned our names without much more than asking."

"Professor Reeves was Prospero?" I asked. "Ariel's father?"

"Yes," Ariel said.

"And what about you?" I asked, turning to the woman I loved. "Do they know your name?"

"Yes," she said, "but they don't know it."

"Eh?" I said blankly. "Go through that once more. 'They know it but they don't know it'?"

She shook her head. "It isn't a good thing to talk about—even to think about."

"But what is this name business?" I asked. "Does it have to be all your names, or just your first name or just your last name, or what?"

"Your real name," Uriel said, and when I looked puzzled he continued. "The name that is you. In most cases, it is your Christian name, although in many primitive tribes all over the world the child is given a secret or sacred name which is known only to himself and his parents."

I chuckled. They looked at me as if I had lost what little sense I had displayed up to now. "That's me. The child with the secret name. I'm not as bad off as we thought. 'Casey' isn't my real name. And I don't think anyone has used anything else since I was christened."

"Thank God!" Ariel breathed.

I took her hand and squeezed it.

"You said you had a clue?" Uriel said quickly, perhaps hoping to head off another demonstration of affection.

I fished out the ticket again. It was getting a little battered. "Maybe. I found this in the little room behind the stage in the Crystal Room. But I don't know what possible good it can—"

But Uriel already had looked the ticket over carefully. Now he balanced it on his fingertips and muttered a few words. The ticket fluttered like a butterfly about to take off. "It fits," Uriel said, looking up. "I'm certain Solomon held this ticket in his fingers at one time. And of course it's natural he should be from Washington."

"Washington?" I echoed. "Why Washington?"

"That's where the power is," Ariel said. "And he is the most ambitious man I have ever known."

"Sure," I said, "where else could he manipulate events so easily and still hide among all the other manipulators? But he could be anyone from a public figure to a power behind the throne."

Ariel's hopes plummeted.

"That makes it difficult," I said, "but not impossible. I've got an idea."

I picked up the telephone, dialed the long-distance operator, and then asked for Jack Duncan at the Associated Press Washington newsroom. I turned to smile at Ariel. She and Uriel watched me hopefully but without understanding.

"Jack?" I said finally. "Casey. Yeah, fine, fine. Well, it's a long story, and this is business. Yeah, important business. Tell me, who's gone from Washington?"

"Oh, man, you've started drinking early in the morning," Jack said sarcastically.

"Come on, Jack. You know who I mean. Who important is gone right now?"

"Everybody, boy. Nobody hangs around here over the weekend but us wage slaves."

I was silent for a moment, frustrated, and then I thought of another way to approach the subject without telling Jack enough to convince him I was really drinking. "Answer me this, then: who is the luckiest man in Washington?" I could see by Ariel's face that she was onto what I was trying to do.

Jack wasn't. "Me, boy," he said. "I start on my vacation Monday."

"Come on, Jack," I repeated. "Who thinks you're important besides your wife?"

"Listen to the man talk! That just shows how little you know my wife."

"Think, Jack!" I said impatiently. "I'm not playing games. I really want to know. Who is the luckiest man in Washington?"

"Don't you even tell me whether it's animal, vegetable, or—?"

"Someone big. Someone you'd know about."

"Lucky?" Jack said. "At cards, love, or horses?"

"All of those, maybe, but especially in getting whatever he wants and wherever he wants to be. And that's maybe the top of the heap."

"Well, well." Jack was thinking now; I could hear wheels starting to spin. " 'Tain't the Great White Father. The honeymoon is over, and he don't like it so good. The word is going around that he won't be running again. And as for the rest—hell, man!—there's only one boy that fits your description. Never seems to need money. All of his enemies have bad luck, but he comes up out of the cesspool smelling like attar itself. And in the last year or so all his intraparty rivals have died or retired with ill health or something—"

"His name, Jack, his name." I was excited now, and I could see Ariel and Uriel tensing.

"You know it, boy." His voice dropped. "Names are dangerous." ("You're telling me!" I muttered.) "Get more people in trouble than any other thing. No telling who might be tapping this line. And I'm not superstitious or anything, but funny things have been happening to people who weren't careful about using this particular name."

"Give me a clue, Jack!" I said eagerly. "I have to be sure."

"America's biggest, bestest, one-man self-help organization," Jack said softly. "Look in today's headlines or yesterday's or tomorrow's. You'll see his name, and never anything but the best things associated with it. There's no doubt about it. The party might not like it, and a lot of Americans might feel like leaving the country, but he's gonna sweep the convention unless somebody fixes his little red wagon. And he'll probably get elected, too. Now that's private stock, boy! Don't spread it around, or if you do don't let on where it came from."

"Got it!" I said exultantly. "He's out of town now, isn't he?"

"Him?" Jack hesitated. "Wait a second." I could hear him yelling something indistinct over the teletype clatter to somebody across the room. "Sorry to disillusion you, sonny," he said. "The great man was seen this morning taking a brisk walk around the block with his cat."

"His cat?"

"Yeah. He's got the biggest, meanest-looking Siamese you ever saw." Jack sounded disappointed. "Sorry. For a moment there I thought you might be going to do the American people their greatest service."

"Thanks, Jack," I said dully. "Can't think of anybody else in his class, can you?"

"There ain't nobody in his class, son. They're all dead or behind bars."

"Okay, Jack," I said. "Let me know if I can do anything for you."

I lowered the phone gently into the cradle and turned slowly to Ariel and Uriel. I shrugged, trying to hide my disappointment. "I guess you heard. It was a thought, anyway."

"Don't get discouraged so easy, son," Uriel said, and his eyes were sparkling. "You've got him."

"I guess you didn't hear after all," I said. "He was seen in Washington this morning."

"Yes?"

I snapped my fingers. "Of course. He flew back to shake off any possible suspicion."

"Could be," Uriel said, "but I don't think so. Too risky switching back and forth. More chance somebody would spot him coming or going and ask questions."

"Well, then," I said, "he could just cast a spell—"

"It's possible," Uriel said, "but then why would he have an airline ticket? No, I have the feeling that the Magus doesn't trust himself to spells any more than he can help. There's always a smidgen of danger and sometimes there's little to be gained."

"What then?" I asked helplessly.

"A simulacrum," Ariel said.

Chapter 13

We and the cosmos are one. The cosmos is a vast living body, of which we are still parts. The sun is a great heart whose tremors run through our smallest veins. The moon is a great gleaming nerve-centre from which we quiver forever. Who knows the power that Saturn has over us or Venus? But it is a vital power, rippling exquisitely through us all the time. . . .

Now all this is literally true, as men knew in the great past and as they will know again.

D. H. Lawrence, Apocalypse

"A what?" I asked.

"A simulacrum," Ariel said again. "A duplicate. Well, not exactly a duplicate. It looks like the person and can do certain simple actions as instructed, but it can't act on its own initiative."

Uriel nodded. "He could have left somebody in disguise, but there's nobody he can trust with his real identity. So he has to do it the hard way. He can assign a few minor jobs, but he has to do all the big things himself. That's his weak point. That and his lust for power."

"And overconfidence," I said, thinking back.

"Maybe," Uriel said.

"Then we've got him!" I said.

Uriel gave me a reproving glance. "We have some evidence, but we can't proceed on this kind of guesswork. We must have proof. It still might be the wrong man."

"What loss?" I said, and shrugged.

"Casey!" Ariel said.

"What do you expect him to do?" I asked disgustedly. "Come up here and present his birth certificate? For magicians and witches, it seems to me that you two are awfully particular. But don't mind me. I'm just a novice at this thing."

"You don't understand," Ariel said firmly.

"The greater the power, my son," Uriel said, "the greater the responsibility."

"That ain't the way I heard it," I said. "The greater the power, the greater the corruption."

Ariel turned her back on me. I could see from the set of it that I had gone too far.

"Look," I said. "I'm sorry if what I said offended you. But after we've got a lead like this, the first break in the case, and you aren't going to make use of it—" I took hold of Ariel's shoulders and tried to turn her around, but she seemed to be made of stone. "Ariel," I said softly. "I'm sorry. I'll go along with whatever you say." I reflected ruefully, as I said it, that she needed no magic to control me.

She looked back over her shoulder. "Well-l-l," she said and turned around to face us.

"You've been jumping to conclusions again," Uriel said patiently. "We aren't going to throw this away. There're some things we can do without endangering any possibly innocent third party. This, for instance."

He rubbed out the circle I had drawn on the rug and chalked in another one. He started inscribing equations around it. After a moment he hesitated and rubbed his forehead. "My memory isn't as good as it used to be," he said apologetically. "I wish I had that book. Must have lost it somewhere."

I bent down and lifted the corner of the rug and pulled out his manuscript. "This?" I said.

"Yes, yes," he said happily. "Dear me, yes. You *are* a help. Where did you find it? Never mind."

He returned to his task, consulting the manuscript occasionally. When he was finished, the rug was almost covered with chalk marks. "There!" he said triumphantly, getting creakily up off his knees.

I looked at it dubiously.

"It's an old Chaldean spell. An exorcism, expressed in contemporary mathematical symbols," he explained. "In cases like this it's helpful to recite the verbal equivalent."

He entered the circle and lifted his face toward the ceiling. Little, white-haired, cherubic, he was not my idea of a magician; he was more like a professor about to expound upon some dull fragment of learning. I wondered again whether I should have rested my fate in his uncertain hands.

Then he began to chant. He had a low and surprisingly effective voice.

"He who makes the image, he who enchants, the evil face, the evil eye, the evil mouth, the evil tongue, the evil lip, the evil word . . ."

Shivers ran up and down my back. This was potent stuff.

"Spirit of the sky, exorcise them! Spirit of the earth, exorcise them!

"The Magician has bewitched me with his magic, he has bewitched us with his magic;

"The witch has bewitched me with her magic, she has bewitched us with her magic;

"He who has fashioned images corresponding to our whole appearance has bewitched our appearance;

"He has seized the magic draught prepared for us and has soiled our garments;

"He has torn our garments and has mingled his magic herb with the dust of our feet;

"May the fire god, the hero, turn their magic to nought!"

I let out my breath. I realized that I had been holding it for a long time.

"My goodness," Uriel said, "I feel better already."

He looked better. The pallor beneath the rouge had changed to a healthier pink. As a matter of fact, I felt better, too. My neck had been sore and stiff. I touched it tentatively. Now it seemed as if I had never had an encounter with an enchanted towel.

"What now?" I asked.

"Now," Uriel said vigorously, "is the time for the counterattack. We must trick Solomon into showing his true face, or revealing his real name."

Silently I pointed toward the back of the mirror leaning against the wall.

"Ideal!" Uriel said. "Now, where would be the best place? I'm afraid the Crystal Room is out. Someone innocent might get involved."

"How about his rooms?" I suggested. "He won't be expecting us to come after him."

"*His* rooms?" Ariel repeated.

"The penthouse," I said, and shrugged. "I may not be much of a detective, but I learned that much."

"The very thing," Uriel said. "I don't know what we'd do without you, son."

"But will he be there?" Ariel asked. Her lower lip trembled a little. I liked to think she was leaning on my courage—or foolhardiness.

"There's one good way to find out," Uriel said. He turned to me. "A program."

I pulled my program out of my coat pocket. "It won't do any good, though. Only the program for October 30 was included."

Uriel opened the booklet to its middle. "Oh, no. This is fine."

I looked over his shoulder. The page that had been headed October 30 had been changed completely.

OCTOBER 31

10:00 THE ORIGINS OF ROODMAS (WALPURGIS NIGHT)
10:30 WHEN THE GOD WAS KILLED—A PANEL DISCUSSION
11:00 EINSTEIN'S FIELD THEORY—A VINDICATION OF THE ART

"Oh, dear," Uriel said. "That was my lecture. I'm afraid there will be a gap in the program."

"After yesterday," I said, "somehow I don't think they're expecting you."

11:30 THE CABALISTS—RITER THAN THEY KNEW
12:00 A SPELL FOR ADONIS
12:30 USEFUL WAX IMAGES AND HOW TO MAKE THEM
1:00 RECESS
3:00 WHY THERE WERE NO PROFESSIONAL MAGICIANS IN EGYPT

"No magicians?" I said.

"All priests. It was the state religion."

4:00 INVISIBILITY—A LOST ART
5:00 THE VAMPIRE IN MYTH AND FACT

"Oh, dear," Uriel moaned softly. "Darker and darker."

8:00 BANQUET
11:00 INVOCATION—PENTHOUSE

"I thought the invocation always came at the beginning of events," I said.

Ariel shuddered. "Not this kind of invocation," she said.

"Oh, me," Uriel said. "Do you suppose—?"

Ariel nodded her head grimly. "I'm afraid so."

"Then," Uriel said with determination, puffing out his chest, "we'll have to stop them."

"What's all this about?" I asked, but they were looking at each other in distress. I shrugged. Apparently it was another of their arcane understandings that I would share when the time was right. I glanced at my watch. Five minutes after ten. Only five after ten? I shook it, but it was still running. "According to the program, then," I said, "Solomon should still be in the Crystal Room and will be for more than two hours yet."

"But how can we be sure?" Ariel asked. Clearly she wanted to take no chances of blundering into the malevolent magician on his own territory. I didn't blame her; I wanted no part of that either.

I picked up the telephone and asked for the Crystal Room. I listened to the phone ring at the other end, and then someone picked it up and said, "Hello," very softly. I could hear someone speaking in the background.

"The Magus, please," I said.

"Oh, I'm sorry," the voice replied. "He's on the stage now. I can call him to the phone if it's urgent, or I can have him call you when he's free."

"Never mind," I said quickly. "I'll get in touch with him later." I turned to Ariel and Uriel. Uriel was chalking equations on the back of the mirror. Ariel was looking at me expectantly. "Let's go," I said bravely. "Let's go beard the magician in his penthouse."

But my knees were shaking.

Uriel stepped back, inspected his work, and pronounced it finished. He turned to us. "You two will have to go ahead. I must attend to some other preparations. Take the mirror and place it where he won't see it until too late. Then search his rooms for some clue to his identity. Failing that, try to get some hair or nail clippings. My friends in Greek used to say that even Homer nods. Why not Solomon?"

I pulled the automatic out from under my arm and inspected it again before I replaced it.

Ariel watched me, and as I looked up she was frowning. "That won't do you any good," she said.

"That's where you're wrong," I said. I patted the lump under my coat with affection. "Maybe it won't do Solomon any harm, but it sure makes *me* feel a lot better."

I got a towel out of the rack in the bathroom, handling it a little gingerly out of memory and respect, wrapped the mirror in it, and turned toward the door. "Ready?"

We took an elevator to the thirty-fifth floor. The elevator had one other occupant when we got on—a large, middle-aged matron with purple hair who stared at the towel-wrapped square under my arm as if she was sure we were making off with the hotel's property. But she didn't say anything, perhaps because we were going up; she got off at twenty-nine and stared after us until the doors closed.

At the thirty-fifth floor we got off and climbed a flight of fire stairs to the penthouse floor. I cracked the door an inch and peered out. The hall was empty. We crept along it, hugging the wall, until we reached the door. It was just opposite the elevator. So far nothing had happened. Probably we could have taken the elevator clear to the top and no one would have known.

All this uneventfulness was hard on my nerves. I watched the shadows suspiciously, ready to jump—for the stairs—if anything moved. I wasn't cut out for this kind of work.

I put my hand on the cold, smooth doorknob and tried to turn it. The door was locked. I looked at Ariel inquiringly.

She muttered something under her breath and reached out with one finger to touch the knob. Nothing happened. The knob still wouldn't turn. Ariel frowned and bit her lip. "There's a spell on it," she said.

I searched my memory for the section of Uriel's manuscript headed "Counter-spells." I reached in my pocket for the piece of chalk that had become standard equipment, drew a circle around the knob and an *X* across the keyhole, and hesitantly jotted down an equation. As I finished writing the last figure, the door clicked and swung gently open.

I turned to smile proudly at Ariel. She smiled back and said, "You continue to surprise—"

She stopped in the middle of what she was going to say,

and her eyes got big. I saw fear mirrored in them as they looked over my shoulder at something behind me. I spun around and stopped, unable to move.

In the doorway, facing us, blue eyes glinting, tail lashing wickedly back and forth, was a tiger.

Even as I identified it, I knew it wasn't a tiger at all. There never was a tiger with a black face, ears, and paws, and fur the color of cream. This was no tiger. This was a Siamese cat, but it was as big as a tiger, and its crossed eyes studied us hungrily as it crouched a little closer to the floor, getting ready to spring. . . .

Chapter 14

She may be promised her life on the following conditions: that she be sentenced to imprisonment for life on bread and water, provided that she supply evidence which will lead to the conviction of other witches. And she is not to be told, when she is promised her life, that she is to be imprisoned in this way; but should be led to suppose that some other penance, such as exile, will be imposed on her as punishment. . . . Others think that, after she has been consigned to prison in this way, the promise to spare her life should be kept for a time, but that after a certain period she should be burned. A third opinion is that the Judge may safely promise the accused her life, but in such a way that he should afterwards disclaim the duty of passing sentence on her, deputing another Judge in his place.

Heinrich Kramer and
James Sprenger, Malleus Maleficarium

"A familiar!" Ariel breathed.

The paralysis of fright left me. I made the fastest draw of my life. The .45 was pointed and my finger was squeezing the trigger when Ariel put her hand past my arm, her finger aimed at the cat, and muttered a few words. Suddenly I was aiming two feet over the cat's head. It had shrunk to normal size. I eased my finger off the trigger and put the gun away, feeling foolish.

"We make quite a pair," I said, "me for the locks and you for the familiars."

"Let's hope nothing comes up we can't handle between us," Ariel said, moving past me. She bent down to pet the cat, but it stared at her haughtily, sniffed toward me, and moved aloofly away on business of its own. I was just as happy to see it go. I let out a sigh and discovered that I was still hugging the mirror under one arm.

"I don't think I'm ever going to get used to this," I said. "Let's get it over with."

Ariel nodded quickly, uneasily, and started across the lush living-room carpet, blood red and glowing in some spots from the morning sunlight slanting through venetian blinds. She headed toward two doors that opened off one end of the room. I looked around for a place to spot the mirror and finally decided on a window. One of the venetian blinds was partly raised. I unwrapped the mirror carefully and propped it in the window frame. The bottom of the blind kept it from falling out.

I stepped back and admired my placement of it—from a discreet angle. If the man who called himself Solomon didn't return until night, and there was good reason to think that he wouldn't, he would never suspect that one window was a mirror until too late.

I hoped that he would get trapped in it as I had.

Ariel came out of one room empty-handed. I pointed out the mirror so that she would be careful. She nodded.

"Find anything?" I whispered. There wasn't any reason to whisper, but that was the way I felt.

She shook her head. "No papers. Nothing," she whispered back. "I've never seen a place so clean. If it hadn't been for the spell and the familiar, I'd have thought we were in the wrong apartment."

She vanished into the other room. I poked around the fancy living room, lifting cushions, peering under furniture, searching desk drawers. I couldn't even find any dust or lint. It was impossible that anything could be so unlived-in.

Ariel came back. "The bedrooms are spotless," she whispered. "Even the sheets have been changed."

"It's impossible," I said. "Nobody could live here even a few hours without leaving some kind of trace. You're right—if it weren't for the cat— Come to think of it, where is the cat?"

Ariel shook her head. "I haven't seen it. That's strange, isn't it?"

My nerves were beginning to vibrate from being stretched taut too long. I was ready to admit defeat and try something else, but there was one more door. We walked toward it together.

"Those were bedrooms?" I asked.

She nodded. "And a bath."

"No personal things?" I said. "No razor? No toothbrush? No deodorant or aftershave or—"

The look on her face was sufficient answer, but she said, "Just unused glasses and towels and unwrapped soap."

We went through the last door and into a small kitchen. It was all butcher-block wood and glass and stainless steel. It looked and smelled as if it had never been used. Everything glistened and gleamed. There weren't any dirty dishes or glasses. No food or bottles in the refrigerator. The place was fantastically, implausibly clean.

I snooped through the cabinets and drawers without hope. Dishes were stacked neatly, glasses were turned upside down, silverware was perfectly aligned.

"If this is magic," I said, in a futile attempt at levity, "someone ought to package it and sell it to housewives." Ariel didn't smile. I said, "Where *is* that damned cat?"

It wasn't in the kitchen, either. There was nothing in the kitchen that didn't belong there except Ariel and me.

Then the cat meowed loudly from the living room. We stiffened. I put one hand on Ariel's arm and with the other hand pushed the door of the kitchen open. The cat was sitting in front of the hall door, looking up at it expectantly. I held Ariel back, as if I could protect her from what was standing in the hall outside the door. But I felt suddenly chilled.

There was a noise from the hall, distant and uncertain, like doors sliding. The cat looked at us and back at the door as if to say, "Now you'll get what's coming to you for breaking into my home." I looked at the cat, thinking that I should have shot it when I had the chance. Ariel peered over my shoulder and whispered, "How can you shoot a cat?" I glanced at her. I knew I hadn't said anything.

We all heard it then: a key slipping into the keyhole and turning.

"Meow-w-w!" the cat said. *"R-r-reow!"* it warned.

The door swung open. I pressed Ariel back into the kitchen and let the door close to a slit. I pulled the .45 out of the shoulder holster and held it ready in my hand. Maybe it was useless, but it felt good there. I heard Ariel muttering behind me. Or maybe she was praying.

And Solomon stepped into the room cautiously, looking at both sides of the door and at the floor. The cat jumped at him, clawing his black pants and talking angrily, in words even I could almost understand, about strangers who had broken into the penthouse, who had violated the sanctity of the place that had been left in its charge. . . .

Solomon seemed to be listening only casually. His head, slowly turning, swept his gaze around the room. He half-turned, his left arm straightening suddenly in a savage arc that sent something in his hand hurtling away from it. Involuntarily my eyes followed the object. It struck. Glass broke. A square of night shivered itself into black fragments that tinkled to the carpeted floor.

But just before the black mirror broke, shattered by the heavy key, I saw Solomon as he really was. The momentary glimpse was enough. I knew him. There was no mistake possible. But it was late for the information. I prayed that it did not come too late.

I looked back toward the door. Solomon was gone. My heart skipped a beat, and then started again, strongly, hopefully. Had the black magician been trapped in his own black mirror before it broke? Had the key he threw shattered Solomon himself into a thousand shards? For a wonderful moment I let myself believe it.

Then, in back of me, Ariel shattered my illusion. She gasped. I swung around, my gun ready.

We faced Solomon. He leaned, dark-faced and smiling, against the stainless-steel sink. The cat rubbed against his black pant leg, its crossed eyes almost all pupil as it stared at us malevolently.

"So," Solomon said urbanely, "the beautiful witch and the intrepid detective." Cream-colored fur lifted on the cat's back; it growled deep in its throat. "Baal!" Solomon said. "You mustn't be inhospitable to our guests, even if they did arrive a little early, and without waiting for our invitation." He looked back at us. "So nice of you to come to see me. You saved me endless trouble in searching you out, and I did want to invite you to my little party this evening. Especially you, my dear." He bowed mockingly to Ariel. "There is a special place in the ceremony for a virgin, and you know how difficult it is to find virgins these days."

"Don't move!" I said, shoving the automatic at him, my finger tightening on the trigger. "Don't lift a finger to work a spell or mutter anything! The first suspicious word or action, and I shoot. Without remorse!"

"But I've already said 'Pax Sax Sarax,' " he said. "That's a sure defense when staring down the muzzle of a gun. In any case, you must realize that if Ariel's spells are useless that thing you're holding is merely a toy." He looked at Ariel. "You can stop muttering now. Nothing will work here except what I will. I put in too many hours of preparation." He smiled broadly.

Anger was a red tide rising in my throat. My finger got white. The hammer clicked futilely against the cartridge. It clicked again and again. I stared down at the automatic in dazed disbelief. It was my last defense, and it had failed me.

"There, now," Solomon said gently. "That was unfriendly of you, and murderous, and unwise. Now I must take measures to make certain that your bad impulses do not overcome you again. In fact, I think it would be better if you did not move again."

As I looked up from the automatic, I froze into place, unable to move, unable even to twitch an eyelash or prevent a tear from welling out of the corner of my eye. Only my chest expanded shallowly, automatically, to draw in air, and my heart kept beating even though it felt leaden within my chest. I could see, however, and by straining I could see Ariel. She, too, was rigid, like a statue of the loveliest woman in the world.

The tear rolled down my waxen cheek.

"Now," he said, "I'll have to put you away until tonight. I must get back to the meeting." He turned to me and smiled. "But thank you for calling and letting me know that you were on your way up."

I cursed my eternal stupidity. When would I learn how to behave in this strange, magical world? Never. It was too late to learn. *But why,* I groaned inwardly, *did I have to involve Ariel as well? I could have left her behind. I could have come on my own.* But I knew that I wanted her with me, because I was weak and afraid, because I wanted her to help me and protect me, because I was afraid to let her out of my sight.

Night came like blindness. I had a moment to wonder if I would ever see again before the light came back. I was in a bedroom, standing, immobile, in the center of the room. I could see the corner of the yellow satin coverlet on the bed and the sunlight coming through the venetian blinds onto the gold carpet. I could not see Ariel. She could have been behind me, and I would never have known, since I could not move my head and she could not speak, but I had a feeling that she wasn't in the room.

The room was large. It had damasked chairs and tables and lamps, and a door that led, apparently, into a bathroom. I remembered that the penthouse had two bedrooms.

Somewhere a door opened and closed. I could still hear and see. That was good. I would not have wanted to be blind and deaf while I waited for my fate to arrive. But I felt a bit like a caterpillar paralyzed by a wasp waiting for its larvae to consume me while I still lived.

I endured the silence and the uncertainty as long as I could. I'll admit that wasn't very long. I struggled against my invisible bonds, if one can struggle without moving a muscle, by willing myself to move, to break free. It was useless. Finally even the will wore out. I felt as if I were sagging inside a frozen husk.

Ariel, Ariel! I thought, unable to call out to her. *Where are you?*

Here. It was like hearing a cool, quiet voice inside my head. Ariel's voice.

Ariel! Is that you? I'm not just dreaming?

Yes, Casey, it's me.

Then it's telepathy. I'm hearing your thoughts.

And I'm hearing yours.

Have you always had it? Telepathy, I mean?

Not until just now, when you called. I think it must be a kind of compensation, a natural ability brought into use by our circumstances.

Where are you? I'm in a bedroom.

In a bedroom, too. The bed has a dark green coverlet.

Mine is yellow.

That's gold. You're in the other bedroom of the penthouse suite.

Are you all right? He didn't hurt you?

Oh, no.

Can he hear us?

No. He's gone.

Her mental coolness surprised me. It shouldn't have. She was a woman of great courage and fortitude. She had been frightened, but she wasn't frightened any more. The worst had happened, and now she wasn't afraid. I was the one who was afraid.

Can you do anything? I asked.

No. I've been trying.

We're trapped then. We have to wait for them to return, for whatever they intend to do with us.

Yes. But she didn't sound hopeless.

Uriel!

Yes.

But Solomon will be watching for him.

Uriel knows that. Don't underestimate him the way, I hope, Solomon will. In spite of his appearance, Uriel is very clever.

Let him be clever now, I prayed. *Ariel?*

Yes.

What is your real name? I want to know. You said that Solomon knew it, but he didn't know that he knew.

It's Ariel, she said. *Father said they'd never suspect the completely obvious. Like the purloined letter, they'd keep looking for something hidden.*

My name's Kirk, I said. *Kirk Cullen. K. C. Casey.* There. We had shared the one thing in this world of magic that meant more than anything else. Well, more than almost anything else. *I love you, Ariel.*

I love you, Casey. The sweetness of it poured through me like wine. I longed to take her in my arms and hold her there forever, but I could only stand stiffly like a statue—a statue of ice with a melting heart.

Ariel, I thought wildly, *we've got to get out of here.*

Yes! she thought, and I knew that she felt the incredible

wonder of it, too. Now that we had found it, this love that knew no barriers between hearts, that let them meet and speak directly to each other, it would be the worst kind of waste to let it be taken away.

Uriel, I said, after another tussle of will against the paralysis that held me, *Uriel will rescue us.*

And so, while we watched the shadows creep across the floor, we shared our most intimate of thoughts and memories like gamblers doubling losing bets until what we stood to lose was unbearable.

Finally we heard a door open.

Uriel! It was an explosion of relief, and I think we both thought it at the same moment.

And then we heard the bland voice we hated.

"Put him down here," Solomon said.

Our hopes dropped with the body I heard lowered onto the bed beside me. The door closed.

"Still silent, old man?" Solomon said. "Well, we'll put you away now, and put you away for good a little later. For good," he repeated with relief. "You've caused me more concern and more trouble than all the rest put together."

Then I heard Solomon leave the room. By straining my eyes beyond the point I had thought possible, I could see Uriel on the bed, small and pale and stiff. He didn't stir. Even his eyes were motionless and blank.

Is he there with you? Ariel asked.

Yes, I answered hopelessly.

I can't reach him, Ariel said, and there was panic in her thought. *What has Solomon done to him?*

The same thing he did to us, apparently, only he doesn't have the telepathic ability that we developed. I didn't try to reach her again for several minutes. Then I asked suddenly, *What did Solomon mean when he mentioned virgins?*

I don't know, she replied. But she knew. She didn't want to tell me, and I didn't ask her again. I didn't really want to know.

We stood, unmoving, and watched the shadows creep across the floor toward our feet like fingers of the approaching night.

Chapter 15

The universe, or Cosmos, is an immense organic being, all the parts of which are interlinked. It is the Macrocosm, or Great World, in contrast to man, who is the Microcosm, or Little World. All the parts of the Great World are subject to the same laws; they function in similar ways, and it is thus easy to arrive at comprehension of them by means of analogy, "Divine Analogy," the universal law which governs all beings. That which is above is like that which is below. The lower is like the higher. In consequence, whoever knows one part of the Macrocosm knows, by analogy, all the parts. He also knows the Microcosm, which is like the Macrocosm and has a corresponding part for every like part of it. The adept can thus arrive at a perception of hidden things not known to the vulgar by the synthetic method put at his disposal by the universe itself, and this method raises him to such a height of knowledge as makes him almost a god.

Grillot de Givry, Witchcraft, Magic and Alchemy

The darkness was virtually total. Clouds must have covered the sky as the night came, because not even starlight entered the room, and I could not see Uriel on the bed or even the bed itself. The carpet was a black pool at my feet, and it almost seemed to me that I could feel myself sinking into it.

We had been listening to voices in the living room for some time now. We had heard furniture being moved around, preparations of some sort being made for something that was about to happen. Something terrible. But the bedroom doors were closed, and we couldn't see what was being done.

I had heard distant thunder. Now lightning flashed outside the room, and a brilliant stroke lit it for a moment with awful clarity. I saw Uriel lying on the bed as stiffly as when he had first been placed there. He hadn't moved since it turned dark, as he hadn't moved before. He might be dead. The thunder rolled. If I could have moved, I would have shuddered.

Ariel! What's going to happen?

Something bad. Something evil. Solomon has been building up to this moment for a long time. With the covens and the black magic. And now it's November eve. We should have suspected why he picked this date for the convention.

Why? Why November eve?

It's Allhallow Eve, Casey. We call it Halloween, but it's no time for children's tricks-or-treats. It was one of the traditional special festivals for witches, a time for invocation and obscene rites, a time for summoning Satan himself, in the hope that at last he would break free of all restraints, he would triumph and assume his rightful throne, the mortal earth itself.

No! I tried to shout, for now I knew with terrible understanding the nature of the ceremony that lay ahead.

Oh, Casey! The door is opening. They're coming for me. They're picking me up. They're carrying me away!

A scream rang through my mind, and I struggled desperately against the paralysis that held me unmoving. Futility surged through my mind. I couldn't stir a finger. I couldn't close my eyes. All I could do was listen helplessly as Ariel's broken thoughts transmitted to me a scene of horror made vivid by her panic and my anguish.

The living room was changed. Ariel scarcely recognized it as two men carried her into the dark room, lit only by tall tapers and the intermittent flickering of lightning that came now through the windows open to the night. The penthouse, I realized, was a new Brocken, a modern "exceeding high mountain" from which to see the kingdoms of the world and the glory of them and be tempted.

They carried her through the room toward an altar draped in black at the other end, where Solomon waited, black-robed and Satanic as shadows changed his face from one demonic image to another, seeming now to give him the look of a wolf and then an ape and then a goat with horns. And behind him the candlelight cast an even larger shadow upon the wall, a shadow that seemed to lurk and loom, to approach and retreat, but always to seem ready to materialize into something more evil than Solomon himself.

There were others in the room. Their dark faces slipped past Ariel on either side, but she recognized only one, the magnificent Catherine La Voisin, who smiled knowingly at Ariel and winked.

Ariel's overwrought senses felt other things in the room, devils perhaps or demons or the spirits of the restless dead. She could not see them, but she could feel them crowding the room, pressing close as if to share in what was about to happen.

On a tripod in front of the altar was a copper dish. In it charcoal burned, making the air shimmer just above it with heat and a trace of smoke.

The men ripped off her clothing. The knit top came off in

raveling shreds; the slacks split down the side seams. The underclothes were torn from her body, and then they lifted her and placed her face up on the altar. All she could see now was the shifting face of Solomon towering above her, looking down at her with evil delight, smiling, his teeth gleaming sharp and ugly and sinister. . . .

Casey! she moaned. Her thoughts were terror itself.

The room was silent except for the thunder that came at intervals like the roll of giant drums, distant but getting nearer. Solomon's head lifted, and he began to speak in a low voice. Ariel could not make out the words at first, and then slowly his voice grew louder until at the end it rivaled the thunder.

". . . gathered here in the required numbers, we summon Thee, Prince, Ruler of Darkness, Lord of Evil; your worshipers summon Thee to receive our sacrifice. We summon Thee by our allegiance. We summon Thee by the great Names of the God of gods and Lord of lords, ADONAY, TETRAGRAMMATON, JEHOVA, TETRAGRAMMATON, ADONAY, JEHOVA, OTHEOS, ATHANATOS, ISCHYROS, AGLA, PENTAGRAMMATON, SADAY, SADAY, SADAY, JEHOVA, OTHEOS, ATHANATOS, *a Liciat* TETRAGRAMMATON, ADONAY, ISCHYROS, ATHANATOS, SADY, SADY, CADOS, CADOS, CADOS, ELOY, AGLA, AGLA, ADONAY, ADONAY . . ."

Casey! He's got a sword! And there's something coming. Something evil! Something terrible! I can feel it. I can feel it getting closer!

Her silent screams echoed and reechoed through my mind. I made one last, convulsive effort that broke my unseen bonds like rotten ropes and sent me hurtling to the door. I tore it open.

Far across the room was the altar with Ariel's white body outlined against its blackness like innocence against sin. Behind her was Solomon, his face looming almost disembodied above the black robe, lit by the red glow of the charcoal fire in front of the altar and the tall candles and the lightning that flickered beyond the windows, almost within the room itself. But the face of Solomon seemed to glow from within with a dark light.

Behind Solomon, cast like his shadow against the wall, was a towering shape of darkness that appeared to draw in upon Solomon as I watched, in upon Solomon and Ariel waiting helplessly on the altar as Solomon's hands lifted the sword high.

"Stop!"

The shout froze the room into a fantastic tableau. But it hadn't been my shout.

Someone else was moving toward the altar, coming into the light of the tapers and the charcoal fire. It was Catherine La Voisin, her hair gleaming brighter than the fire. And then, suddenly, it was no longer the red witch. Uriel stood there, where she had been. Small, old, shabby, he defied the room.

"Begone, shadows!" he said, pointing one long finger toward Solomon and the altar. As he pointed a spear of light shot out from his finger. "Flee, shadows! As you must always flee before the light!" His body seemed to glow in the darkness. "Twisted projections of a twisted mind, vanish into the nothingness from which you came!"

He rattled off a series of equations, filled with functions

and derivatives, faster than I could begin to follow. But I felt a fresh, clean wind blow through the room, like the wind that follows the rain as the cold front passes. Cobwebs and old superstitions seemed to be swept away. Ariel stirred.

The shadow behind Solomon had shrunk when Uriel's finger of light struck it. Now it dwindled further, seeming almost to crouch behind Solomon.

"Go!" Uriel commanded.

Solomon awoke as if from a daze. "Night conquers the day," he thundered. "Darkness conquers the light. Power makes all men bow before it. Then *bow!*"

The sword over Ariel trembled in Solomon's hands as he fought to bring it down, to complete the awful sacrifice that would complete the victory of evil, that would complete the bridge that would allow the Lord of Darkness to cross over into our world. Solomon's Satanic face and black figure towered over Uriel's white-haired insignificance. They battled for the sword, the two of them, straining against invisible forces.

Slowly the sword started down.

"Senator!" I shouted.

Solomon looked up. He peered across the room toward me, trying to see who was speaking, his face contorted with effort, beaded with sweat.

"This time the gun will not fail, Senator!" I yelled. "The bullets are silver, and your name—your real name—is written on them!"

I pulled the trigger of the gun that had rested in my hand for more than twelve hours. My hand recoiled again and again. I saw his robe twitch. He staggered. The sword drooped in his hands. And then slowly, certainly, it lifted again.

The hammer clicked emptily.

"Lights!" Uriel shouted. "Let the light chase away the darkness!"

Blindingly the lights came on. The young man who had been doorkeeper of the Crystal Room was blinking dazedly beside the switch. But all the others in the room seemed just as dazed.

Uriel's finger was outstretched now toward Solomon himself. His lips moved rapidly, but I could hear none of the words because thunder was rumbling through the room. Energy flashed, brilliant, electrical.

Lightning seemed to pour down the blade of the upright sword. The sword fell harmlessly to the floor. There were no hands to hold it. The black robe crumpled to the floor. There was no one inside it.

Solomon was gone.

I heard a door opened and the sound of running feet, but I didn't look to see what was happening. I was racing toward the altar, toward Ariel. I gathered her into my arms and kissed her and held her tight. She was crying shakily, but in a few moments her arms went around me, and she stopped trembling.

"Casey!" she said softly. "I knew you would save me."

I wanted to savor the occasion, to keep her gratitude all for myself, but I couldn't. "It wasn't me," I said. "It was Uriel."

I half turned. Uriel was standing beside us, smiling mildly, looking pleased but not triumphant. Otherwise the room was empty; the others had fled.

"It was mainly trickery," he said, grinning sheepishly. "To confuse Solomon, because he believed in such superstitions." He opened his hand. There was a pencil flashlight in it. "That was the beam of light. I used a phosphorescent dye on the clothes and by hypnosis induced the young man by the light switch to smuggle in an ultraviolet projector. The most difficult job was immobilizing La Voisin." He shuddered. "A most uncouth and violent woman."

"What about Solomon?" Ariel asked, shivering as she turned to the black robe crumpled on the floor behind the altar.

"Oh, he's gone," Uriel said cheerfully. "Where I haven't the slightest idea. But he won't be back. I hated to do it, but he kept insisting on forcing his warped ideas onto formless energy. When I turned that back upon him, he was, so to speak, consumed by his own demons. Now that he's gone his simulacrum in Washington will die in a few days. A neat ending for public consumption, although something of a puzzle to the doctors, no doubt." He looked at me approvingly. "Those bullets were very helpful. They distracted him at a crucial moment."

"They didn't seem to do much damage," I said ruefully. "Of course they weren't silver, and they didn't have his name on them."

"Wouldn't have helped if they were," Uriel said. "In that pile of clothes I think you'll find what in my day was called a bulletproof vest. He always liked to play both sides."

"You gave us such a scare, though," Ariel said. "We thought Solomon had captured you."

I turned quickly and raced to the bedroom door. "My God, yes!" Uriel was still lying there on the bed. I looked back and forth between the two of them. "I don't understand—"

"Solomon wasn't the only magician who could create simulacra. I knew it would be a bad moment for you two, but it couldn't be helped. I let him take this one, and he didn't even wonder why it was so easy. He had a bad habit of underestimating his opposition. But I'd better get rid of this."

He muttered something under his breath. The image disappeared, and the mattress rose where the image had lain.

I sighed. "Now we can forget the whole thing."

"Forget!" Uriel exclaimed. "Dear me, no. The Art is still valid. It must be given to the world."

"But—but—" I spluttered, "that would be like telling everybody how to make atomic bombs in their basements!"

"Concealing it would be like destroying the steam engine," Uriel said sternly. "Knowledge can never be suppressed, young man. Common understanding is the finest safeguard against misuse. Of course there are some finishing touches that are necessary. Oh, dear me, yes. I must be going. There is so much to be done."

He nodded happily to us and trotted out of the room.

I turned to Ariel. She had slipped back into her torn clothing, which I found almost as fetching as her nakedness. She fumbled behind her back, looking at me over her shoulder.

"Don't worry, Casey," she said. "He'll be putting finishing touches on his theory for years. Fasten this, will you?"

I fastened it, and it seemed very commonplace and

marital, but it sent shivers up and down my arms, and this time it wasn't terror.

"I wonder what my life will be like," I said, bending down to kiss the soft hollow between her throat and her shoulder, "when I'm married to a witch."

She took a deep breath and leaned her head back against mine. "It's a good thing you said that. Because you haven't any choice. From now on you're going to be a faithful, submissive husband."

"Why?" I asked uneasily.

"Because," she said, twisting around to press herself against me, "I know your real name."

I sighed and resigned myself to my fate. After all, every man marries a witch, whether he knows it or not, and I would never love her any more than I did at this moment. Even better, I would never love her any less. That's one of the blessings of magic.

But all this was years ago, and I think Uriel is getting restless. He thinks the Art is finally ready, and he wants to reveal it to an unsuspecting world.

So any time now—if you should see a book called something like *The Mathematics of Magic* or even an obscure article in a mathematical journal, or if you should find yourself madly in love with a girl you've only met, or if you should walk into a hotel and discover a convention of magicians . . .

Brace yourself! The age of magic has just begun.